# THE
# HERO OF ST. LO

## stories of Abbeville
## and the Upcountry

**Benjamin Wirt Farley**

*Illustrations*
Felix Bauer

Jacobs Press
Clinton, S. C.

Library of Congress Cataloging in Publication Data

Farley, Benjamin W.
    The Hero of St. Lo: stories of Abbeville and the upcountry.

    1. Abbeville District, South Carolina—Fiction. 2. Anderson County, South Carolina—Fiction. 3. South Carolina—History—Fiction.

I. Bauer, Felix Karl, ill. II. Title.

PS3556. A714H4                                           83-81867

to
Margaret,
John,
and
Bryan

# TABLE OF CONTENTS

# Preface

The stories in this collection are the result of a proud and historic county's impressions upon an imagination that has long loved the South and whose roots are anchored in that mystical and metaphysical reality which the South inspires, even in the last quarter of the twentieth century.

The first stories were shared with Bill and Cindy Kibler and Louise Ervin of Honea Path. My association with them resulted in the publication of "The Hero of St. Lo" and "The Angel Tree" in the *Anderson Daily Mail,* of which Mrs. Ervin is a staff writer. For the encouragement this gave me, I am indebted to each of them and to Tim White, at the time an editor of the *Daily Mail.*

I am also grateful to many others: Miss Kathryn Galloway of Due West whose reminiscences inspired "The Old Hotel"; Charles Plaxco and Robert Gettys, also of Due West, for the title "The Graveyard Covey"; the Rev. James F. Pope, pastor of the Flat Rock African Methodist Episcopal Church, Antreville, for the theological and political insight that gives "Ride to Louisville" its sense of realism; Fred West, editor of the *Abbeville Press and Banner,* whose gracious assessment of the stories was most encouraging; Felix Bauer, professor Emeritus of Art, Erskine College, for providing exceptional illustrations; and, above all, Dr. Wilbur H. Reames, Jr., Associate Professor of English, for reviewing the manuscript and suggesting many helpful changes.

Benjamin W. Farley
Due West, South Carolina

# THE
# HERO OF ST. LO

# The Hero of St. Lo

On the Court House lawn of Abbeville, South Carolina, rises a handsome monument to the memory of "The Major of St. Lo." The granite marker commemorates the bravery of one of Abbeville's proudest sons. It also stands as a reminder of the tragic price that many a family and small town have paid in time of war.

On July 17, 1944, battalion commander Major Thomas Dry Howie led his troops in a successful attack against the German forces that had made St. Lo the eastern hinge of their battleline. In an effort to join forces with another embattled battalion of the 116th Infantry Regiment, his battalion finally cracked the German line. Howie himself was killed by a mortar shell in the ensuing German bombardment.

St. Lo was taken the following day, July 18, 1944. The Major was dead, but General Charles H. Gerhardt, commander of the 29th Infantry Division, ordered his body carried through the rubbled streets in an ambulance and had it placed in state on a pile of toppled wall beside the church of Ste. Croix. Against the background of artillery fire, thrown up by the retreating Germans, the troops of Howie's division passed in solemn review.

The granite marker on the Court House lawn was erected by members and friends of Howie's family and dedicated in his honor in a quiet ceremony some five years later. On the face of the smaller, left side of the monument the following words are inscribed:

Major Thomas Dry Howie
1908-1944

Commander 2nd Battalion
116th Infantry, 29th Division
U.S. Army

3

The new stone gleamed in the warm sunlight of that first fall. The cold crystals of winter frosted its edges until the morning sunshine dissolved them. Cool spring rains beat against its crisp lines and letters, sacred to the memory of the Major's loved ones.

Then one humid, July afternoon, a sudden shower having drenched the square, leaving trails of steam to evaporate above the brick pavement, a lone figure made his way to the stone. The man knelt in the wet grass and observed a long requiem before the hero's monument.

Passers-by were stunned to observe this public act of sorrow. Clerks in the Court House grouped about the doorway and watched in surprised silence. Necks craned for a better view.

Even shoppers on the west side of the square caught sight of the mourner's form and stopped to stare in curiosity. "Why, have you ever?" "Imagine that!" "Who can he be?" "Isn't that sad!" "Isn't that odd!" "Isn't that brave!" Etc.

Many of the onlookers were tenderly moved by what they beheld. Some gawked in silence. One or two wagged their heads in disapproval. Some smiled and nudged each other nervously. But none who saw it could forget the humbled form, oblivious to the traffic and anxious glances of the town.

As suddenly as the man had appeared, he rose to his feet, bowed in silence one last second before the marker, then turned and disappeared down Pickens Street.

An old Negro farmer, sitting nearby on a park bench, had risen unconsciously to his feet and was still standing silently at attention before he realized the stranger was gone. "Whew, Lawd!" he exclaimed. "Lawd, Lawd!" he repeated, flashing an embarrassed smile.

The word soon spread over town. Ministers referred to the incident in their Sunday sermons. Bridge clubs made it the topic of their conversations. Then, as days drifted by, the town tucked the visit quietly away in its memory, and life continued as usual about the square.

Exactly one year later, to the date—though no one realized it for several days—passers-by were startled when the same figure reappeared and repeated the identical ritual.

Many new shoppers on the square had much the same reaction as those who had witnessed the event a year earlier. People strained to catch a glimpse of the man.

Men, women, and children alike crowded the island around the fountain or gathered in groups about the Confederate monument. All stood with their hands clasped in front of them, as if mourners at a funeral, and shared the stranger's grief or gratitude, or remembered Tom as they had known him.

Many automobiles stopped or slowed to a respectable crawl.

Who was this man? One could only assume that Major Howie had played a prominent role in this man's life, and now he came in pilgrimage to this shrine to pay homage for that act. No doubt he must have been a member of Howie's battalion who had fought by his side on that fateful road to St. Lo.

No sooner had the man arrived, it seemed, than he stood up, brushed off his trousers at the knee, walked to a parked car nearby, and drove away.

"Did anyone see who he was?" people asked. "Yes!" came a volley of replies. "He was tall and had dark hair and one ear was missing."

"No, no! He was short with blonde hair and wore glasses."

"Yes, with a red moustache! No doubt Irish!"

"Not at all! He was frail and frightened. He looked Jewish to me."

"Bosh! You wouldn't recognize your own mother! He was muscular, wiry, rough-looking, athletic!"

"I beg to disagree! He's an army chaplain. I'd know him anywhere. I'm sure he's the man who helped bury the dead at the Laurents Cemetery."

Etc., etc.

The third year the square was packed. One of the reporters for *The Press and Banner* had managed to confirm that the second visit occurred on July 18—the day of St. Lo's capture. He, therefore, reasoned that the first visit likewise occurred on the same date and speculated that the stranger would appear again the forthcoming July 18. Throughout June and early July *The Press and Banner* featured special articles on the Major and mused about the recent incidents.

The crowd that gathered in Abbeville that third year was primed with curiosity and eruptive with excitement. Several veterans' groups were on hand. Flags decorated the square. The high school band had been concealed in the Trinity Episcopal Church to march out at a moment's notice. The mayor had stationed himself near the

Court House. Two of the city's policemen had volunteered to seize the man, if necessary, so that the city might learn his identity and express its admiration of him. Everything was set.

Since he had come before about mid-afternoon, no one actually expected him until after 2:00 or 2:30. By noon, however, noisy groups of shoppers and crowds of curious persons had congested the square. Traffic had to be rerouted and parking space was at a premium. Any stranger driving into Abbeville that day would be sorely tempted to bypass the city and return another time.

This became apparent to the publisher of *The Press and Banner* as early as 11:00 A.M. when scarcely any walking space remained about the square. When by 3:30 the mourner had not appeared, everyone's disappointment was evident.

For the most part the crowds behaved respectfully. A few incidents erupted here and there. A hot-tempered fist-fight was quickly cooled when one of the pugilists fell into the fountain. Everyone laughed.

By 4:30 half the throng had left and by 6:00 only a few diehard groups maintained their vigil. By 8:00, they too departed.

The mayor and town officials had retired to their homes by 6:30. Only a few late strollers remained on the square. By then, the veterans' groups had departed, the flags had been recased, and the band long since thanked for its willingness to parade and, with appreciation and regrets, sent home.

Twilight draped the square. It would soon be dark. The first stars of evening twinkled above the night. The air stirred with cool breezes. The grass grew wet underfoot. And then the stranger came. He parked his car near the Court House, hardly anyone paying him attention. He got out, walked to the lawn, and knelt again beside Major Howie's monument.

The man's few witnesses stopped where they were in the darkness. They strained their eyes to note every detail. But, as had been the case with others in the two previous years, they were so moved by his act of piety that their own hearts were stilled and each offered up his own quiet prayer. Night engulfed them all in its starry glow.

The man returned to his car by streetlamp and drove away.

Other summers came and passed. Every July the stranger kept his self-appointed watch. Never again did the town mount a surprise welcome to wrest from him the secret of his mission or learn his name. They let him come and go and stood quietly with him about the square while he fulfilled his self-commissioned vigil.

Once again it was July. The stranger stood beside the marker. His hair was gray. A look of unbelievable anguish marred his face. He steadied himself against the monument with his left hand, bent his knees stiffly, and knelt to stare at the Major's name. He leaned his head forward against the stone in silence.

Now throughout these years there had been one man—a merchant—on the square who had witnessed all the visitations. At first he had watched them with unbelief, even sarcasm, as he too had fought in the Second World War.

Had he not landed that same dreary June day on those same cold, fearful beaches with the rest of the 116th Division? Had he too not hugged the wet sand and listened to the chatter of enemy fire? Had he not also crawled and sprinted across endless fields and flung his rain-soaked body into hedgerow after hedgerow? Had he not seen men disintegrated by mortar bursts and dismembered by weapon fire?

Who had not died for others in battle? What soldier did not know that ultimately indifference toward death is his only antidote for fear?

What toll the price of a single battle! 1,818 of their own division for the rubbled mound of St. Lo. Had not the 30th Division lost 3,934? That was three out of every four, wounded or killed. Or nine out of every ten in the rifle platoons.

"The battle of the *bocage*," Bradley had called it. "Breakout!" "COBRA!" But "Death" or "Hell" would have been sufficient.

Yet as the years had crept by and the stranger had returned to keep his lone and solemn vigil, sarcasm had given way to guilt and guilt to a deep sense of remorse. As the merchant stopped his chores to stare, he recalled a moment that flooded him with pain and forever made him one with the stranger across the square.

It was not at St. Lo but several kilometers beyond. His company had been joined by a detachment of French Irregulars who had volunteered to guide them through the hedgerows.

He could still remember the German grenade—a "potato masher," as the G.I.s dubbed it—that had suddenly been hurled into their midst and had rolled between his own feet. Too stunned to react quickly enough, he had begun to emit a loud wail of terror, when one of the young Frenchmen suddenly seized it and arched his arm back to fling it away. He could never forget that Frenchman's face! Its delicate, angular features and olive complexion would haunt him forever.

The Frenchman's act of courage snapped his spell, and as he lunged for cover, he was half hurled there by the grenade's explosion. As he rolled to his side, he could hear the dying man's moans. *"Aie pitié de moi, O Dieu!"*

The man's comrades tearfully surrounded him and, cradling him in their arms, bore him away.

As he remembered the incident, tears burned the edges of his eyes, and he hoped no one saw him raise his hand to hide them. He suddenly wished that there were some unknown and secret tomb by which he might just then kneel and also pray, "Have mercy on me, O God!"

The stranger had finished his watch. He rose awkwardly to his feet and glanced about himself. Then, instead of returning to his car, he crossed Pickens Street, then South Main at the corner of Lomax's Hardware, and came up the bank and department store side of the square. People stared in unbelief as the man passed by.

The merchant had stepped outside his store and stared too. The stranger came closer and closer, occasionally glancing into the shop windows or nodding respectfully at onlookers.

The merchant could tell that the man's right hand was maimed and that his face was deeply scarred. Just then the two men's eyes met. Less than ten steps separated the two.

The stranger raised his arms. *"Mon ami!"* he called aloud, as the merchant fell at the Frenchman's feet in a violent sob of tears.

---

Note: Factual materials for this story are based on articles by Hal Boyle in *The Press and Banner* (Abbeville newspaper) and Omar Bradley's book, *A Soldier's Story*.

# RIDE TO
# LOUISVILLE

# Ride to Louisville

The September air was dry. The gum trees at the edge of the lot had already begun to turn red. Fall was in the wind.

Dust covered the wild grapevines and honeysuckles that edged the woods. Shafts of broom sedge nodded gently in the warm breeze. Overhead, the orange sun broiled down hot upon the dusty road and dry yard.

The Rev. Carington Jones mopped his forehead with his hand and glanced at his watch. It was 12:30 p.m. Time to leave.

He walked slowly toward his car, slid into the driver's seat, and closed the door. His ponderous frame betrayed the physique of a once mighty gridiron tackle. Now he was 52.

His '73 Olds started smoothly. He backed it out of the drive. He aimed his car south and began the ride to Louisville. As he passed several of his black neighbors, he raised his large hand, waved amiably, and smiled.

Somewhere deep inside his hulk, his soul ached. For the past two months, he had sensed himself slipping into despair. "And that isn't good," he acknowledged aloud to himself.

He passed his A. M. E. church. "The church where you pastor," he corrected himself. How its clapboard sides needed painting! Even the letters on its sign were illegible. But he drew invisible power from its quiet walls and plain glass windows.

He thought of the choir in their new blue and gold robes. With the eyes of his mind he surveyed the young and the old, the weary and the expectant faces of his congregation. In his reverie he addressed them:

"We have come to worship God. Who among us is not weak? Who among us has not suffered? Who among us has not been afraid? My brothers, my sisters, let us open our hearts to the Almighty in prayer."

"Yes, brother. Yes, Lord," he could hear them say. "Amen."

He waved to a group of black children at the end of the block. "That's our preacher!" one little girl shouted. "Preacher Jones! Preacher Jones!" the children shouted.

They waved to him as he pulled out onto the highway. He waved again, then settled back for the drive.

Twenty minutes later he neared Abbeville. Rather than take the bypass, he decided to drive through town.

He slowed for the traffic lights at the square and passed the Confederate monument on his left. Several brothers sat on benches under the shade. They were old men and seemed oblivious to time or change. They laughed and seemed to enjoy one another's presence.

It made him smile and feel good.

He glanced up at the monument. He had read where the Klan was active in Alabama again. "Why? Why do they want to do that? And in Florida, too."

All the dark images of night riders and burning crosses rushed to his mind. He struggled inwardly to dispel them.

"Why can't the big evangelists stand up and speak a clear word? Why won't they tell their people it's wrong?" It posed such a big question in his heart, that he shook his head in disappointment.

He thought of the passage in Acts where Peter saw the heavenly sheet filled with all the animals. "Peter, do not call unclean what God has called clean."

Poor Peter! The Lord had to lower that sheet three times before Peter understood that God is for all races. "If only the evangelists could see that, too."

He thought of Stokely Carmichael's words, or whoever it was that said them. "I'm Black and I'm proud. I'm Black and I'm somebody."

"Yes, Yes!" his heart affirmed.

He drove toward McCormick and Plum Branch.

The pines that bordered the road seemed to quiet him. There is something lonely about pines, sad and darksome. The occasional dogwoods and gum trees, bright with their first tinge of fall, made him think of the stigmata on the Saviour's hands and side.

He began to hum. "Precious Lord, take my hand, guide me through this weary land. . . ."

His mind wandered.

He passed a large junkyard and used auto-parts lot. A man was repairing a truck by the edge of the road. The yard's many old cars and trucks could be seen behind the tall, limp, dry grass and gnarled scrub oak trees.

Suddenly an idea for a sermon was sparked in his mind: "God's Repair Business!" Life is so broken down. So many old and rusted parts. While the Devil Inflation smiles at the poor man. What's a brother to do? Take your life, brother, to the Lord. Take your life to the "Almighty Repair Shop." Maybe that would do, but he would have to give it more thought.

His mind wandered again. . . .

A shanty beside the road brought him back to reality. A vestige of the cotton era, it was. And there was a sister, sitting on the porch, watching the children in the yard. Like a page out of *Uncle Tom's Cabin.*

South of McCormick, and again at Plum Branch, he passed busy log yards with railcars stacked with cords of pulpwood. "What would we do if it weren't for lumbering?" he thought.

In sections of South Carolina, that was his people's only trade. "Only means of livelihood and dignity," he said aloud.

The poor black! Always the last hired. No way to earn seniority. Always the first laid off.

If only he could totally trust the white man. If only the black man could feel that he had a friend in the white man, then whenever issues of justice and humanity needed to be applied, the black man could sleep at night.

How proud he was of Theo Mitchell—Chairman of the Black Caucus! Now there was a erudite humanitarian. Yes, there was much to hope in and for.

Those prepositions "in" and "for" reminded him of what he planned to preach on Sunday. The Parable of the Sower and the Soil. "Some fell 'on'; some fell 'among' and some fell 'into.' God wants to put his love and will 'into' our lives, not simply watch it fall 'on' us or bounce in 'among' the thorns. But 'into'!" he repeated, as he slapped the dash.

He passed a group of brothers clustered about a small gas station. They reminded him of the corner at home.

How many "corners" must America contain? Corners where the brothers get drunk, cut one another up with knives, shoot off steam?

But how else can the oppressed show their manhood, except by taking it out on themselves?

A cream-colored pickup truck, flying a Confederate flag from its radio antenna, pulled around him and cruised on down the road. He stared hard at the flag. "The white swastika," one of his young deacons called it. Like the skull on a label of a bottle of poison.

He knew that flag was the symbol of a proud and rebel South for many whites. He could understand that. But why couldn't they understand that for the black man it symbolized the status quo, the old ways, the old traditions, the unchanging when humanity cries out for change?

He wished he had the courage to fly a big white banner from his car. He would want nothing on it but the words of Micah 6:8:

> What doth the Lord require of thee,
> but to do justly, and to love mercy,
> and to walk humbly with thy God.

He crossed the dam at the Clarks Hill reservoir. The bright water of the lake sparkled in the sun. The air was clean, the blue sky clear. The hills of Georgia rose up softly beyond the Savannah—flowing restlessly below.

How pure and good and cleansing it all seemed! "I will lift up mine eyes unto the hills. From whence cometh my help? . . . ."

He tried to envision God. The God who created those hills and piled up the water of the Red Sea. "Indescribable" was the only word that came to mind.

As he drove across the dam, he imagined himself riding on the fatherly edge of God's invisible hand. God was holding back the waters for him. The thought inspired his heart with hope and peace.

He felt reverence toward God. He didn't want to hurt God. "Why does everyone want to hurt God?" he thought aloud.

He wanted to be quiet. As he drove along the highway, he thought of the 23rd Psalm. He could picture David's bountiful table and see the shepherd-king sitting there in peace, while his enemies looked helplessly on.

The imaginary scene, as he drove down the highway, protected by its pine and hardwood forests, filled him with new zeal and courage.

At Harlem he stopped at a Zippy Mart for gasoline and a soft drink.

14

He solemnly slapped hands with a young brother and listened to the palaver of the old men. He glanced at his watch. Time to drive on.

The airport at Wrens captured his interest. He counted two small crop-dusting planes. A large field of cotton dominated the landscape.

He took the back road into town. He drove by the rusted metal buildings of the old cotton gin. Then he drove by the A. R. P. Church where Erskine Caldwell's father had once been pastor.

*Deep South* was the only book of Caldwell's he had ever read. He liked the way Caldwell had paid homage to his father. He could respect a white man like that.

He knew there were many whites like Caldwell's father. If there hadn't been, the black race couldn't have come as far as it had.

The manse was still there, opposite the church. He slowed as he drove by it. The shade of its front porch looked so inviting. But there was no time to linger.

Between Wrens and Louisville, he marveled at the well-cultivated fields of soybeans. They stretched for acres across beautiful, cleared farmland.

The fields reminded him of harder times, near Anderson, where he had grown up as a boy. His parents were dead. They had been sharecroppers and had worked for the greater part of their lives on a single impoverished farm.

He shook his head. It was still a mystery to him how any of them had survived that era. Especially the poor.

Just inside the city limits of Louisville, a white policeman stopped his car. The officer was halting traffic for the blue buses of a private academy to gain access to the highway.

He had to wait for all the buses to come out. All the children on the crowded buses were white.

After the vehicles had gained access to the road, the policeman let the traffic continue its progress. As he drove on downtown, a stream of yellow public school buses passed him on its way out.

The buses were only half filled. All their riders were black. The smaller children seemed swallowed up inside the big, whale-like buses.

At last he parked his car by the square at Louisville. He rolled down the windows and left it unlocked. Then he walked toward the old slave market, established in 1798, but now restored and in picturesque condition.

15

He stopped outside the open-air mart to gaze at its original timbers and wooden shingled roof. He looked up at its quaint cupola. The rooster, on the weather vane, was pointing south. His tall feathers pointed north. The Reverend smiled. He guessed it would always be that way.

He stepped inside the market and welcomed the cool of its shade. He ran his hand over one of the great supporting timbers.

Here, in 1863, his own grandmother had been sold as a slave. She had always wondered why Sherman's soldiers had not burned the market down to the ground. She guessed they were too occupied with tearing up the railroad and getting on to Savannah.

He walked over to the bell—the bell that rests on its iron mount in the center of the floor. He had read its inscription many times. It had come from France in 1772. Intended for a convent in New Orleans, its ship had sunk near Savannah, and now it rested here.

How ironic that the nation that had given America the Statue of Liberty had sent this pretty bell to grace the lives of nuns in Louisiana, only to have it wind up in a *slave* market in Georgia!

He beheld it with reverence. Then he said softly to himself, "I have never forgotten you, grandmother. Nor the long road our people have travelled and climbed. You have ever been present in my thoughts. You have never been absent from my soul."

He sighed. He reached his hand forward and ran his fingers over the side of the old bell. "O gracious God," he whispered. "Never again need we be sold as slaves. Thank you, Father. Thank you, God Almighty."

He gently pulled the clapper back in his hand and let it strike the opposite side of the bell. The clean, sharp sound of the bell rang out across the square. He smiled and rang the bell again.

He listened as its clear tone echoed up under the roof and filled his heart with new hope, memories of love, and the courage of freedom.

He did not turn to look back as he walked to his car. He opened the door, climbed in, and closed it. He was ready to return home.

# LONG CANE
# PLANTATION

# Long Cane Plantation

On a narrow winding road near Abbeville, obscurred behind old cedars and gigantic elms, looms a proud vestige of better years. Slivers of light play gently on tall, moldering, white-washed columns —six in all—that support a once elegant porch with two balconies above it. Behind that lofty facade rise three octagonal sections of house, with their large octagonal rooms, joined by long and spacious hallways.

Coming upon it as suddenly as one does, a stranger will almost veer off the road, staring at it in unbelief. Known as the Long Cane Plantation, one can readily imagine what it must have looked like in its days of glory.

Dense woods of pine and oak lurk about the house. A high board fence with a mesh-wire gate obstructs a clear front view. A sign warning sightseers to keep away guards the sandy lane that leads back to the house.

One can understand the sign. For who would not love to own this proud estate or have the money to restore it?

At an intersection opposite the house stands an old stagecoach inn. In its prime, it accommodated up to forty guests. Now, of its original twenty-two rooms, only five remain. In this scene of bustle and chatter, its hostess set one plate for each toll of the bell the ferryman rang when the stagecoach crossed the Upper Long Cane Creek less than a mile away.

About two hundred yards from this inn, on the old highway between Augusta and Abbeville, one passes the Elm Grove A. R. P. Church. Partially hidden behind a graceful magnolia, the present sanctuary was erected in 1853. Its dark, handmade brick create a feeling of antiquity and piety, befitting the church's venerable heritage.

A large cemetery separates the church from the road. Many lichen-stained tombstones stand vigil over the lawn. Strangely, in the midst of a crowd of gravestones, lies a wide unmarked plot. One is struck by its clean and well-kept appearance. Perhaps slaves are buried there, one muses. But it is late, and work remains to be done in Abbeville and Anderson.

Some say it all began in the 1760s. But long before Scotch-Irish settlers claimed the land, Indian tribes camped throughout the Long Canes. Their clashes with and occasional "massacres" of the immigrants are a part of South Carolina's distinguished past.

In fact, it was rather late in history when Captain William Henry Bradley of Charleston acquired his 1,200 acre plantation along the Upper Long Cane and began building his three-tiered, veranda-fronted home. Being a retired sea captain, he brought his own ship's carpenter with him to design and oversee its construction. Begun in 1845, it was not completed until 1857.

Reminiscent of his seafaring days, Bradley had his men install octagonal portholes along the hallway of the top floor. Banistered steps then led up steeply through an attic, where latched doors of a cupola opened out onto the roof and a narrow walkway.

Here the Captain would retire for sanctuary whenever he wished to get away. Sometimes on stormy evenings, even in heavy rain, he would pace this deck, as if commanding his former vessel through the restless swells of the sea. When the wind became more than he knew he should chance, he would descend the stairs, latch the doors behind him, and stare out the portholes.

Because of his behavior, most of the house servants were wonderfully obedient. Only the family's long-time slave nurse, Mama Bessie, dared go up to the deck to fetch him.

She'd slip her head out the cupola and shout gruffly above the storm, "Cap-um, suh! Da women an' dem slaves of yo'se is done scare-t to deaf! An' you up here a misseratin' wit da devil! Mizzie done say fo' you to come down, right now, fo' you catch da deaf uh nou-monia!"

The Captain would feign anger and shout through the gale, "The storm will soon pass! Then I'll be down. Now leave me be!"

"Yes-suh!" she would snap, looking warily at him, while she shook her head and mumbled to herself, "Crazy fo' show! Dat man is crazy!"

Only when the house was completed did Bradley move his family from Charleston. He was 58 at the time; his wife, Martha Alexander, was 42; his son, Alexander William, was 19; and his daughter, Constance Louise, was 12. His oldest son, Frazer Henry, had died at sea while on a voyage to England.

Since the Captain had exchanged the wealth of his shipping enterprise for the prosperous farm, all his fortune was now invested in the Long Cane Plantation. And prosperous it was! Its lands yielded bountiful crops: corn, cotton, sweet potatoes, and molasses. Its slaves were of sound health and reasonable morale. Its buildings, fences, and livestock were the envy of neighboring planters.

Typical of the gentry to which he now belonged, he entertained Abbeville District's prominent families and citizens. He hosted parties, soirees, hunts, and, in 1860, even the gala Danse de Noel! Frequent visitors in his home were the Smiths of Abbeville and the sons of the distinguished Perrin family. "Many was the evening" he rented all the tavern's twenty-two rooms for the comfort of his guests.

A South Carolinian by birth, he was present in Abbeville the day the Legislature voted to secede from the Union. In the Spring of 1861, he personally helped James M. Perrin and several planters recruit, uniform, and outfit their Companies for service in Orr's "Regiment of Rifles."

With all the excitement of the hour, he was as pleased to see young Alexander made Perrin's lieutenant as Alexander was to be elected to the honor. How smart they looked in their uniforms! How well they drilled to the bands! How handsome and formidable they posed before the Court House! He could not help joining in the rounds of "Hoorah!"

When just a little over a year later, in June of 1862, it fell the lot of Orr's Regiment to lead the main assault at the Battle of Gaines' Mill, he gathered before the Court House steps, with all the anxiety and grief of others, to hear the latest news.

How saddened he was to learn of Lieutenant Colonel Augustus Smith's death. How relieved he was that Alexander was not among the 81 killed or 234 wounded.

As he listened to the reports, he could fully imagine the terror of that great battle. The thunder of its cannons and musketry! The wild yells of its spirited soldiers! The unit banners flapping and disappearing in the smoke of gun powder! The cries of the wounded and dying!

He attended the long memorial service for Colonel Smith and tried to comfort the widow. When he arrived home, he climbed the steps to his roof sanctuary and paced its deck. He paced for his friends whose sons were now dead. He paced for his own dear son, Alexander. He paced for himself. Back and forth he paced. Then he paced for the Palmetto State he loved and for the gallant armies of the Confederacy.

Mama Bessie was finally sent to fetch him down. She peeked out through the doors of the cupola but could not bring herself to shout.

She wanted to say, "Cap-um, dat's da price of freedom! All dis killin' an' wah!" But instead she cried, as tears filled her eyes, "Oh, Cap-um, thank God Massah Alex is still alive! Remembuh, suh, he's my baby too. Cause I done raised him fo' you an' Mizzie since he wa'nt nothin' but a pup. Ain't dat so?"

She dabbed her eyes with her apron. "But I feels so sorry fo' dem other white folks, cause they done lost dere boys fo' evuh!"

The Captain bent down and took her hand. From that day forward, a bond was knit between them that could never be broken.

When eleven months later, news of Major Alexander Bradley's death—killed at the Battle of Chancellorsville—was carried by rider to the Captain, Mama Bessie screamed with grief and blocked the passage to the deck. But the Captain made no effort to climb the stairs.

Since the "Seven Days' Battle" around Richmond, of 1862, he had expected such news would one day come. Now that it did, it pierced his heart and fell into the void of his soul.

He clasped his arms around Martha, Connie, and Mama Bessie and joined them in their tears. They all moved solemnly out onto the second balcony. Huddled together, they wept in turn: one in their sorrow, one in their loss of Alexander, and one in their love.

"O Daddy," sobbed Connie, "if God is fo' our side, why can't he stop this wah? Why won't he make those Yankees sue fo' peace?"

How could he tell her what he knew was a certainty now?

Later that evening, after everyone had finally retired tearfully to bed, he stole away to the attic. He climbed the steep stairs. He unlatched the doors and stepped out onto the deck, aglow in the milky radiance of the moon. He paused by the banisters for a moment, then knelt in the heavenly light, slumped to the deck, and held on to the rails with all his might.

From below he heard the faint wail of Mama Bessie. He could never forget what she said.

"O Lowd, Lowd! My onlyest white baby! Is das da price of dis old slave's freedom? O Lowd! He done sucked da milk out of dese very bosoms, long wit my own. He done be sanged to sleep by dis old voice in dese same black arms."

She moaned in sing-song fashion. "If das' da price of freedom, Lawd, I humblies 'cept it, though it break dis old mammie's soul!"

The Captain rolled onto his side and stared blindly at the moon.

The "Abbeville Press" Friday, May 15 paper offered some consolation, but at best it was a tribute to a doomed and faltering cause. Colonel James M. Perrin, commander of Orr's Regiment, had also been killed at Chancellorsville. The editors tried bravely to honor the two bereaved families.

In a reference to both officers, the editors wrote:

*These noble-hearted, lofty-minded men of Orr's regiment, have fallen a sacrifice to patriotism, whose duties they knew so well and illustrated on so many fields of battle. It is a matter of deep regret to record the fall of the brave and the young. Some of the most gifted, talented, and worthy men of our district have now fallen, and this list only adds to its number.*

The Captain read on:

*The sympathy of the whole community flows to Col. Perrin and Major Bradley's inestimable families, who have, in God's Providence, been called upon to sustain life's deepest sorrow.*

The editors concluded with a poem:

*Now may the gates of heaven swing open as high as the sky, To let Col. Perrin and Major Bradley pass by!*

Time heals sorrow's wounds, but war ever inflicts others. The defeat of Lee's armies at Gettysburg signaled the long withdrawal. Vicksburg, Chattanooga, Atlanta fell. Augusta awaited the next blow from Sherman's armies. Orr's Regiment was far away, committed to the tragic cause in Virginia. Abbeville was astir with consternation. Where would "Sherman's Butchers" strike next?

It was early December, 1864. Skiffs of fog had already begun to gather, as the cold air of evening mingled with the last hours of day. It would soon be dusk.

Connie stood on the top balcony and looked out across the lawn. "If the Yankees are goin' to Charlotte," she reasoned, "they'll come right up that road. They'll burn the church, the inn, the mansion, ravage the plantation, and keep right on!"

She had read all about the foraging parties—their killings, rapings, and pillaging. "Even dressin' slaves up in their masters' costumes!" She had heard about Wheeler's own corps, too; "Southern cavalry!" —plundering, burning in the path of the enemy, expropriating food, guns, fodder, horses!

Connie wanted to cry. She was nineteen. "A 'groan' woman!" Mama Bessie called her. But she felt no older than a little girl and wanted to cry.

She glanced down in the yard below and relived those dreamy moments of La Danse de Noel. She could still see the handsome beaus arriving for the party, the carriages backed up to the stables, the ladies all powdered and gowned in the latest fashion.

Suddenly, the sound of horses caused her to look up. A string of wagons stretched just beyond the gate. She reached for the nearest column and screamed to the top of her voice, "Mama Bessie, Mama, Daddy! The Yankees are comin'! I see them comin'! They're comin' through the gate, right now!"

In her excitement, she almost fell over the rail. As she caught herself, a lone rider passed through the gates. Behind him, breaking their way through the mist and frosty fog, appeared seven to eight wagons. Terror gripped her heart. Were they Yankees or Wheeler's men?

By the time the rider was close enough to be identified, Connie's fear had given way to shock and indescribable grief. Three wagons had trundled heavily through the gates. Their drivers were reining them up under the trees below. Four more entered slowly behind them. Each was filled with bandaged and wounded men, their uniforms in tatters. Most of the men were without blankets and visibly shivered in the cold.

Even the rider was wounded, for she could see bloodstains on his coat, high on his left shoulder. His trousers were filthy. His boots were white with mud. His coat hung in rags: The initials "C.S." were emblazoned on his cracked and weathered saddle bags.

Just then, the creaking of the wagons ceased, and the groans of the wounded drifted across the cold air. Connie gasped and clutched her breast.

The rider saw her anguish, tipped his hat politely, and painfully dismounted. She could see he was young and unabashedly handsome. She heard her father come out on the porch below.

"Captain Bradley!" the young rider addressed her father.

"Yes," he answered, somewhat cautiously, with surprise.

"I'm Jeffrey Brooks, Captain Brooks, with the Eleventh Texas Regiment. My father said we'd find you here."

"Jeffrey Brooks!" repeated her father. "Why, yes! I don't know what to say!" Then he added quickly, "Where is your father? How is he?"

"Near Augusta," answered the captain. "Still alive, I pray. We've been in some hard fighting. I've got a lot of wounded. As soon as I can, I've got to get back to the Eleventh, just as fast as I can find them."

"Well, I believe that shoulder will come first," replied her father. "But we can talk later. Tell me what's to be done. I'll send for doctors, whatever. I've ample room for all your wounded inside."

The young officer stole a glance up at Connie and smiled. "We're much obliged," he said. Then he lowered his voice and said to the Captain, "Some of the men are dead. We lost them on the road." He pointed to one of the wagons.

"I see," her father said, with sadness in his voice.

It took two hours to carry in and bed down the wounded. Mama Bessie saw that all were fed. Frightened servants scurried everywhere. Connie helped her mother cut away bloodstained cloth and bathe wounds.

Doctor Tilliston arrived from Abbeville and administered what medical relief he could. Long into the night, he dressed hideous wounds and, before morning, had amputated a half-dozen shattered limbs.

Exhausted by the ordeal, he whispered to the Captain, "I wouldn't be surprised if some of these men die. They simply came too far and lost too much blood."

Captain Bradley thanked him and rode back with him as far as the ferry.

Connie found herself embarrassed and yet excited by the attractiveness of the young officer. She had not taken care of herself since Alexander's death, and she knew her face and hair showed it.

Mama Bessie caught her primping in the mirror and spanked her on the behind. "Lawd, chile, you outht ta be eh-shamed of yo' se'f! All a dressin- an' a primpin' fo' I know who! An' him lame in dee arm!" She laughed, her eyes atwinkle.

Suddenly, she hugged Connie and began to cry. "Oh, chile, dis wah is soon be over. I feel it comin'. An' my heart is all con-fused into. Fo' it ain't ever gonna be da way you dreamed, no mo'e. Ain't no way it can en', honey, cept in sadness fo' you. Dat young Jeff-ree boy, he gonna be jus' like massah Alex-sander."

Connie held tight onto her nurse and tried to comfort her. "No, no, Mama Bessie," she partly scolded her. "We aren't gonna let it defeat us, utterly! No, no! We just can't!"

For two weeks, the Bradleys covetously enjoyed the young officer's presence. Connie learned how her father had met him while on a voyage to New Orleans and how later he had met Jeffrey and his brothers, too.

She listened with interest and remorse as he described the black column of smoke that had drifted over Atlanta while the men of Wheeler's corps kept Sherman's armies under surveillance. She grimaced as he refought the skirmiches at Sandersville, Sylvan Creek, and Waynesboro. She could see the corn cribs, cotton gins, and barns enveloped in smoke in the path of Sherman's men. She could hear the noise of the tracks being destroyed and feel the heat from the piles of burning cross-ties.

Names she had only heard about, he used with casual familiarity. Hume's division. Iverson's. Harrison's and Ashby's brigades. The Third Arkansas Regiment. General "Fightin' Joe" Wheeler. Anderson's command. Colonel Cook and his Eighth Texas Regiment. General Dibrell. Etc.

When a fortnight later he left with fifteen others—all mounted and resupplied with horses, food, and ammunition provided by her father and other planters—she hurried to the top balcony and waved farewell. At the gateway, Jeffrey turned in his saddle, waved his hat, and threw her a kiss. She clutched a handkerchief in her hand and cried as he rode away.

Altogether, they buried eleven men. They buried them in a mass grave, on the edge of the cemetery, within a stone's throw of the church. Captain Brooks did not know all their names, for some belonged to regiments and companies of which they were the sole survivors. Two, however, were from Alabama and two from Mississippi. The others were buried unknown.

Today the cemetery slopes off gently toward a driveway. Hundreds of tombstones fill the area between it, the church, and the highway. But one can still see the unmarked plot, green and well kept.

One can also drive by what remains of the old inn. And since there are few cars that travel the road, one can stop and slip out of the car and peer through the gate at the Long Cane Plantation.

A profusion of trees blocks the full view, but beyond the tall elms, crape myrtles, and pecans, one can still see the graceful columns and count the balconies. They are empty now, and all is silent, save for the wing-beats of a pair of doves, frightened into flight, by the sound of your coming.

# A WALL
# OF ANGELS

# A Wall of Angels

No one knew who the man was. All the townspeople knew was that one day the vacant house, midway up the hill of the old estate, surrounded with its ancient pecans and bending live oak trees, had a new resident.

His maroon Packard suggested wealth and gleamed handsomely in the circle drive. Here he parked it under the ivied-limbs of the grandest live oak tree.

Few caught a glimpse of the man. In fact, he rarely appeared in public. Apart from the reticent postmaster, who had met him only once, no one else would have known him had they seen him face-to-face on the street.

For an entire year he lived in this manner, in the way of an eccentric recluse. Then one day he appeared in his yard, slovenly dressed and drunk, and had to be helped back to his house.

The town doctor performed this neighborly act, and, although his curiosity was aroused, the physician dismissed the incident as one of those awkward foibles of life.

Not long after this, masons were seen erecting a high brick wall, which they stuccoed with rough mortar, along the back edge of the estate. Then to everyone's amazement, an exquisite piece of white marble statuary was raised to the wall and cemented in place. It was a magnificent angel!

Townspeople came and stood in the street and gaped at the lovely creature.

"Well, at least, he has an eye for beauty," observed the mayor.

"And a wad of cash to afford that," added the town's engineer.

"Whatever must he do?" sighed a next-door neighbor's wife

"Or have done?" wondered her husband.

"Still it is grand," said the mayor. "In all my life, I have never beheld anything as lovely as that."

"Agreed!" they replied.

Two, three, . . . five years came and passed. Still the townspeople knew the man little better than they had the first day he moved in. Sometimes he could be seen in his yard, sometimes beside the wall. Once he was seen on the wall, sitting beside the angel.

"Could he be crazy?" the mayor asked.

"Or drunk?" the engineer suggested.

"Something can't be right," the neighbor's wife asserted.

"Why not just say he's eccentric?" offered the doctor. "Why jump to pejorative conclusions?"

"And what are 'pejorative conclusions'?" asked the neighbor's wife.

"Negative reactions," explained the doctor.

"Perhaps," said the mayor. "But you must admit, it is odd."

"Yes," everyone concurred. "It is odd."

The very next week the man backed his Packard into a ditch and demolished the left rear fender and tail light. It was raining, so the man simply sat on the running board and waited until someone came by.

Once again, it was the doctor who happened by. And hardly to his surprise, he found the man hopelessly inebriated. "Can't you see you need help?" scolded the doctor. "Let me give you a prescription. Don't you care that you are about to ruin your life?"

The man only moaned and clung helplessly to the doctor as the physician aided him back to his house and returned for his car.

Two weeks later the town was stunned to observe a second majestic angel being raised to the wall. The workmen secured it in place about twenty yards from the first and set the second angel at such an angle that it faced the first. Its graceful wings created the illusion that it was actually aloft. The angel's right hand reached forward, as if longingly hungering to touch the first angel, or something infinitely more sacred and ineffable beyond.

No one who saw it could pass it without staring. The angel evoked feelings that ordinarily remain undisturbed in most of us for life.

"Can you believe that!" some of the town's most hardened hearts uttered.

"I know," came the hushed reply of scores.

On Sunday afternoons strollers would pass by the house just to see the two angels on the wall.

For what seemed like an eternal recurrence, the estate's owner visited the wall every day. He would kneel, first, beside the earlier angel; then, after a long period of meditation, he would walk reverently toward the second and repeat his ritual.

For weeks nothing prevented him from keeping his rounds. Then, one day, he ceased them altogether.

The Packard was never repaired. In time it was driven back up under one of the pecans and abandoned to rust, mildew, and rot. Privet shoots sprang up around it, as well as broom sedge and berry vines. Soon it was covered over and scarcely noticeable.

The owner replaced it with a Buick, which he parked now beside the rusted, front screened-in-porch of his house. How the grand old estate was going down!

"How the man is caving in!" groaned the doctor. "I have never treated anyone like him in my whole life," he confessed to the mayor.

"At least he lets you treat him," replied the town's engineer. "Do you realize, you're the only one who sees him face-to-face!"

The doctor shook his head quizzically. "I know."

Year succeeded year. Except for the physician, the town all but forgot about its eccentric alcoholic. People could not remember when they last saw him. Only a few cared.

"I think he gets his mail at night," said the postmaster. "About once a week I find his box empty."

"Well, I know he doesn't stay in all the time," said his next-door neighbor's wife. "Occasionally, his car is gone."

"Can't you imagine how lonely he must be?" added a friend.

"Or insane," hinted the postmaster.

"Still, I love to walk by his house," acknowledged the neighbor's wife, "and look up toward those two angels. How I wish I might see them close up, or touch one!"

One night this neighbor and her husband heard screams coming from the eccentric's house. They heard the explosion of glass, the tinkling and shattering of windows, or of something glass. It terrified them and created an emptiness in their stomachs. The wife called the doctor while the husband slipped hurriedly next door.

He crept through the tall grass and under the dark limbs of the live oaks and pecan trees. The back door of the house stood open. A yellowish light cast a path into the darkness, illuminating the stucco wall and one of the angels.

Beneath the angel staggered the barely recognizable form of a man. He appeared wild beyond description. He was smashing liquor bottles against a rock while cursing and crying with sobs uninterpretable.

The neighbor crouched in the shadows and watched. He waited until the doctor arrived. The mayor and the engineer were with him. It took all three men to wrestle the drunk to the ground. Then the doctor injected a sedative. Finally, when the man lay still, the three men carried him with effort into his house.

One month later the mayor burst into the doctor's office. With a worried smile he announced that a third angel had been added to the wall and that the recluse was bowing in front of it, weaving to and fro, in abject grief.

"The workmen say they have never seen anything 'so pitiful' in all their lives. One of them says he cried like a baby from the moment they arrived. He even flung himself on the statue and tried to kiss it."

"Very well," moaned the doctor. "I'll come as soon as I can. Keep an eye on him till then."

The mayor did. And long after the doctor had soothed the strange sufferer and had managed to coax him from the wall, the mayor made frequent reconnaissance of the lot to check on the desperate soul.

His conditioned worsened. His alcoholism increased. He began piling his liquor bottles under a mossy pecan tree. The man became a mournful and dismal sight.

Totally unexpectedly he began wandering the streets. The pain in his face was so intense that most people ceased to demean him and actually offered to help him home.

The climax came swiftly one evening, some three years later, on a bitterly cold night in March. Following a heavy siege of depression and a week of near delerium tremens, somehow, in a moment of inexplicable lucidity, he ordered a fourth statue for the wall.

When the statue arrived, he appeared at the kitchen window, drunk beyond human capacity. With a sickening crash, he knocked out several of the panes with a liquor bottle and began to emit an eerie primitive howl. It rose from the fissures of his soul and drifted across the misty pecan grove to haunt the men erecting the latest angel.

In accordance with his wishes, this statue was also placed in such a way that it faced the first. But unlike its predecessors, its face was lifted heavenward. Its arms were outstretched, as if expecting an imminent rendezvous. The wings touched each other back to back. The expression on its face was one of indescribable, aloof and distant peace. A philosopher observing it might have said, "Transcendence."

Suddenly, upon seeing it, the man's howling ceased. Even in his stupor, it was as if he had finally seen and understood what his anguished heart had sought across the years. He waved to the angel and backed away from the window.

That night the sky above his lot became a roaring torch. The man had set fire to his house. Seconds before he perished, however, he was seen fleetingly standing as if to jump from a second-floor window.

"Then he just stepped back on his own," wept the neighbor's wife. "I called to him twice, but it was like he couldn't hear, or was listening to someone else's voice, greater and farther away than mine. That's when he stepped back into the flames."

Several months later the doctor stopped by the lot on his way home from his office. He left his car in the street and walked up through the grass, under the pecan and live oak trees.

He surveyed the ruins of the house. Rats crept out of the pile of liquor bottles and scurried unmolestedly about. "What a pity," he whispered to himself.

He moved on up toward the wall. He walked its length, pausing to meditate beneath each serene and beautiful angel. Then he turned to walk back to his car.

The old Packard in the privet hedge caught his attention. For a reason he could later define only as "Providence," he walked over to the rusted heap and, seeing its trunk door ajar, raised it.

In the trunk he discovered a bundle of folded, old newspapers. They were copies of the *Atlanta Constitution*. There must have been a dozen or so.

He sorted through them, discovering they were all the same issue and had the same date. He picked up one and folded it open. "Oh, no!" he cried. "Oh, Father, no!"

On the front page a terrifying picture captured his attention. The scene was late at night. A luxury hotel raged on fire. A man was falling into the arms of firemen at the top of a ladder. Above him, beyond the reach of the ladder, in a window silhoueted by smoke and flames, appeared a frantic woman with three little children in her arms.

"Oh, Father! Oh, God!" wept the physician. "Oh, God!" he sank to his knees beside the rusted Packard, as he trembled and convulsed with tears.

When the county's tax office auctioned off the estate, the doctor bought the property. He cleared the lot of the charred ruins, the old Packard, and the pile of bottles. Then he added a fifth angel. He had it set beside the first, so that the right hand of the fifth angel touched the left hand of the first.

Sometimes in the evening, when one walks down the street by the old estate, one can see the doctor sitting beside the wall. He sits there so often in sorrow, but, for the most part, he leaves it in strength.

The wall of angels has changed his life. He attends his church with greater regularity than ever before. He is as kind as any man in our town. He has funded five nurse's scholarships, in three different hospitals. He has turned the old estate into a park for all who care to come and meditate beside a wall of angels.

# THE GRAVEYARD COVEY

# The Graveyard Covey

Abner DuBois was a proud Huguenot. His family had emigrated from France to America in 1744 and had settled along the Upper Long Cane Creek of South Carolina. It was an era when the Creeks and Cherokees still roamed the forests, when turkeys and buffalo were bountiful, and wolves and bears prowled at night.

In the early 1800s his ancestors moved to Abbeville, founded and named by still other groups of French emigrants. But after the Civil War, his grandfather settled near the town of DeWitt, where he bought an abandoned and mortgaged plantation on the edge of the quiet hamlet.

The DuBois fortune seemed to rise until the Depression, then the boll weevil and a faltering Southern economy brought its climb to a halt. By Abner's time, only a ninety-acre tract of land remained in DuBois hands.

A dense woods undulated across this tract. Oaks, pines, cedars, hickories, poplars, maples, and sweet gums rose above its leafy floor. An occasional magnolia adorned it here and there.

The land itself lay along a gentle ravine, bounded by a creek to the west and a mile-long field of soybeans, corn, and winter wheat to the east, owned by a prosperous group of Mennonite farmers.

Abner was a printer by trade, an employee of a shop in Abbeville. But he lived in his grandfather's farm house, remodeled and bricked-in, on the edge of the woods, near one of the corners of the large Mennonite field.

His wife, two daughters, and membership in the Donalds Presbyterian Church occupied the greater part of his free time. However, he always managed to reserve one measure of time for himself— quail season in the late fall and early winter months.

He owned no bird dogs, but their absence posed no loss. He could sense a covey's presence, if one were about. He rarely missed a shot.

And he could walk up single quail long after the covey had scattered.

But it wasn't the shooting of the birds that Abner enjoyed. It was ambling slowly along the edge of the vast soybean field with the warm sun to his back, or stalking the field's honey-suckled corners and vine laden fence, and carrying the shotgun across the crook of his arm that pleased him.

In fact, what he loved most was to descend the gentle slope of the long ravine, pick his way through the tall briars and dry vines, listen to the murmur of the creek as it rippled quietly over its gravelly bed, and watch the rays of the afternoon sun angle hazily through the dark woods and somber pines.

What more could a man want? What more did his soul need? *"Alors!"* as his ancestors would have said. "Hasn't God made it so? *C'est magnifique!"* Yes, it was strangely perfect. What more needed to be said? Abner was content.

Now deep in his woods, shadowed by a copse of pines and rounded smooth by weather and the passage of years, rose a series of low and forgotten mounds. Layers of pine needles covered them. Broken cones and decaying pine boughs poked up through the matted litter over them. The forest floor was damp and the woods quiet around them.

"They're Indian burial mounds," his grandfather had explained. "We must never molest them." And Abner never had, nor ever intended to.

Abner loved these woods and this pine copse in particular. He cherished it above all the acres of his land and revered its ancient graves.

He knew quail nested nearby. And more than once he had flushed a large covey in the burial area itself. But he never fired at the covey. For he would not violate the quietness that prevailed here, nor disturb the slumber of its deceased residents.

"Is this not *la terre sacrée?"* he could hear his grandfather say. "Yes, *Grandpère,* it is holy ground."

One day while hunting along the creek, near some thickets and pokeberry vines, he flushed a covey of quail and killed an unusually large-sized bird. His eye marked the spot it fell, while he watched the remainder scatter and wing-off up the ravine, toward the pines.

He squirmed through the briars to retrieve the bird. It was a beautiful male and felt abnormally heavy in his hand. Its craw literally sagged in his fingers from the weight of the grit and seeds it had eaten.

"What a prize specimen you are," he said to the bird. "What a pity your friends have left us!"

With that, he stuffed him into his pouch and hurried on up the ravine. He flushed a second quail, dropped it, placed it in his pouch, and approached the pines with caution.

He knew the frightened remnants of the covey were nearby. He walked quietly along the forest floor toward the mounds. He stopped beside the copse and glanced respectfully across the graves.

The hazy light of the forest filtered through the pines and rose in smoky columns of light above the damp pine-matted covering over the mounds. He would not infringe upon the covey's sanctuary. He felt ashamed that he had pursued them this far.

He backed quietly away, hoping not to disturb them. But as he did, he stepped on a dry bough, and its snap sent the covey into a loud explosive flight.

"Ahh!" exclaimed Abner. "I meant you no harm. I apologize. *Je me regrette.*"

Then he looked across the mounds and addressed its silent dwellers. "I am sorry old friends to have interrupted your silence. Do not be angry with me. I love the peace your pines preserve. I salute you from the edge of this threshold. Peace, my brothers of the forest and children of God's primitive world. He has given you rest. So must I."

When Abner returned home, he stopped by an old shed to clean the quail. First he plucked off the speckled feathers. Then he emptied the entrails onto the ground.

He was curious why the craw of the larger quail felt so heavy. He slit it open with his knife blade and turned it inside out. It was filled with soft metal pellets. They were dark and mossy on the outside. He scraped one with his blade, creating a bright yellow scratch along its surface.

"Gold!" he exclaimed to himself. Could the pellets be small beads of gold?

"*Bon Dieu!*" he uttered aloud. "This can't be!"

But it was. The craw was packed with a dozen or more green mossy globs. Each glittered when he cut it in half with his knife blade.

"Gold!" he repeated. "I can't believe it! *Grandpère,* if only you were here! Somewhere on our property is gold! Can you believe it? Gold!"

He stooped over in the grass and examined the craw and entrails of the other quail. He picked through the grit and half-digested wild seeds. Then he saw them: one, two, two tiny beads of gold.

He re-examined the small pellets. He compared them in size and shape. They were not nuggets. They could not have come from the stream. They appeared to be beads, ancient gold beads.

The mounds! Surely they came from the mounds! He had killed two of the graveyard covey. And somewhere among those mounds. . . .

His heart raced with excitement. *"C'est incroyable!"* he knew his grandfather would have said. He stood up, grinned with joy, and stared at the small pellets in his hand.

What should he do? He decided he would say nothing about the matter to his wife or daughters. At least not yet. They would learn in time. Instead, he would explain that he had lost something in the woods and thought he could return to the spot where he had dropped it.

He put the pellets in his pocket, hurried to the house, rinsed the quail under an outside spigot, and handed them to his wife.

"I lost my favorite pocket knife in the woods," he said. "I think I know about where I lost it. I'll be back by supper. *Adieu,* my love!" he grinned. Then he was off.

"Isn't Daddy crazy at times," said the younger daughter.

"Yes," replied her mother. "He'd live in the woods if we'd let him. But he's a good man."

Abner moved quickly and quietly through the woods. His gun nestled comfortably across the crook of his left arm. He slowed his pace to reload it, then descended toward the pines.

*"Alors!* Abner, what are you doing?" he asked himself in a whisper. "Have you gone *fou?* Unload your gun. Come, now, get hold of yourself."

He sighed, stopped, and eased the shells out of the chamber.

By the time he reached the copse, the sun was setting in a glorious blaze of light to the west. Its soft rouge color diffused through the forest and created a gentle glow over the ancient mounds. A silence as profound as the cold seemed to reign over the graves.

He stopped by one of the great pines, put his hand upon its dark trunk, and stared at the silent mounds. What secrets did they contain? What lost and buried lore lay hidden beneath those worn and weathered humps?

The sun's glow faded, and darkness settled over the woods. The first stars of evening appeared, and heralded the coming night.

Abner felt strangely cold. He shivered for a moment, sighed, turned away, and trudged thoughtfully home. "I will come back tomorrow," he said aloud.

Abner might just as well have not slept that night, for when he rose in the morning, he was restless and weary. What's more it was Sunday.

As they were eating breakfast, his wife asked, "Are you well, Abner? You look pale, worried?"

"I'm fine," he replied.

"Did you ever find your knife?" asked his younger daughter.

"No," he answered softly, ashamed of his lie.

Just then his older daughter came in. She was the prettier of the two. She looked at him with her deep green eyes and, with a casual flip of her head, tossed her long red hair back over her shoulders. "Where did you lose it, Daddy?" she asked.

"I really don't know," he mumbled, as he got up and kissed her on the cheek. Now the lies start, he thought to himself. What will come next?

That morning the worship service dragged. His mind was captive to one thought only—the golden pellets, the glittering globs, those incredible warts from the mounds. If, indeed, they were from the mounds. . . .

His mind wandered throughout the service. Perhaps they were no more than a string of beads from a careless girl's necklace. Anyone could have lost them years ago. But he doubted that.

Perhaps they were fragments from a chest of loot, hidden from the Yankees when the old plantation had been abandoned and Sherman's army was raiding Columbia. "No!" he almost said aloud. "That can't be either."

"Shhh!" hushed his wife. "What's wrong with you?"

"Daddy, be quiet!" grinned his younger daughter

"Shhh!" whispered the older girl. "You are all an embarrassment!"

He listened to the pastor for a moment, but his mind wandered again.

Perchance the mounds were not graves after all. What if they were old wagons? Old wagon beds? Old wagons covered over by time and debris? The lost wagons of the famous "last chance gold"?

Everyone thought that gold, lost during the last days of the Confederacy, had disappeared in the lower part of the state. But why not here? Couldn't the wagons have come back here? Why not at Abbeville? Hadn't it been the scene of the first state's secession and the last meeting place of the Confederacy's Cabinet? What could be more logical?

Still, that couldn't be. No! His grandfather would have known the difference between buried wagon beds and Indian burial mounds.

But what would Indians have wanted with gold? It was only after the Spaniards came that. . . . Of course! The Spaniards! DeSoto's men! Hadn't their whole mission been to locate gold? Yes!

And hadn't their route brought them by this very way? Between Augusta and Anderson? May, 1540? Of course!

Could the mounds then be the graves of Spaniards? A small party of Spaniards, or their Indian guides, who had found gold? *Bon Dieu, Grandpère,* could that be it?

When the congregation rose to recite the Apostles' Creed, he leaped up and affirmed it with such vigor and loudness that his daughters laughed.

"Oh, Daddy!" they roared, after the service. "You are completely *fou!*"

Abner laughed with them and kissed both girls. "I have found my knife!" he announced.

He could hardly wait till they returned home. Once they arrived, he explained that he had lost his appetite for dinner and, scarcely pausing long enough to change clothes, hurried toward the ancient mounds as fast as he could stride.

Once he came to the pines, he slowed his steps. He still revered these woods and cherished the quiet copse. Ahead of him lay the mounds. Through the tall, solemn pines he could count the graves—nine in all.

Somewhere out there, time and the quail, he was confident, had uncovered an ancient pouch, filled with its tarnished pellets of gold. But if only he knew where!

He paused by the trees and gazed out over the mounds. The air was warm. Sunlight filled the space with a lazy shaft of haze. All was quiet, save for the distant caw of a blue jay. Nest robbers, they were.

He felt uneasy. On the one hand, he wanted to search for signs of quail droppings in order to find the covey's nesting site. Yet on the other hand, he didn't want to violate the sanctity of the graves.

What should he do? Should he return home for a shovel and begin unearthing each grave, one by one? That thought was abhorrent, though tempting.

Should he lie down between the pines and wait for the quail to return? He had once stalked a covey that way for almost an hour. They had fascinated him by the meticulous and cautious manner in which they had scratched and advanced their way through a dry honeysuckle thicket. But this was no honeysuckle thicket. And the ground was damp.

Perhaps he should keep coming back, keep returning to the copse, in the hope of flushing the birds over that mysterious spot where he trusted the mosssy globs might be visible?

Maybe he should simply hunt the birds down, kill them one by one, until he had eliminated the entire covey? At least that way he would retrieve part of the booty.

He shook his head. He loved the mounds. How could he desecrate them? He loved the quail. How could he destroy the covey?

He was about to turn and wander back to the house when his eye caught a movement near one of the graves. A quail had peeked its head up out of the pine litter. It suddenly called plaintively. Its delicate cry slipped through the forest and sank into the silence of Abner's soul.

The bird seemed lodged. It tried to flap its wings. It looked up across the forest floor at Abner. It was as if the bird were calling him for help. Then it "beeped" faintly, dropped onto the pine needles, and lay still. Abner was shocked.

He had taken no more than two steps toward it, when he discovered another dead quail at his feet. Here and there he caught the movement of other birds. Their faint cries broke the silence, as each struggled momentarily before it died.

One or two mounted into the air, flapped frantically, then fell crazily, dead.

He could not believe his eyes. Never in all his life! *"Grandpère,"* he whispered, "what is happening? The covey is dying before my very eyes."

Suddenly, he forgot about the gold. A treasure he valued more than he had ever realized was slipping away, dying in his very presence.

When the copse finally grew silent, Abner began examining each bird. He felt their swollen craws. Each was stuffed with the dark motly pellets. He slit one of the birds open with his knife. Its tiny digestive system was ruptured, poisoned by the beads.

"Gold!" he said with disgust. "You have killed my covey. You have killed the dearest creatures that graced these woods."

He turned and gazed across the graves. "O spirits of the forest, forgive my ignorant lust. O Father in Heaven, forgive. I came so close."

He reverently gathered the quail into one large heap. Then he bent down beside it and began covering it with pine needles and debris. When he had completed his task, he stood up and stared across the ancient graves.

As he walked away, a voice deep within him comforted him beyond his own capacity to console himself. *"For where your treasure is,"* the voice said, *"there will your heart be also."*

# "MIS-TUH JAY"

# "Mis-Tuh Jay"

Mrs. Hattie Hawthorn lived in one of DeWitt's grandest homes—
"the Lila Grey House." The old, charming, antebellum mansion still
graces Main Street and, though its grounds are unkept, it is bordered
by wide beds of jonquils and azaleas, rows of yellow-bells, and high
hedges that bush up from behind the house, ending only at the edge
of the front sidewalk. Until recently, the lawn, with its hedges and
flowers, was cared for by an old negro gentleman, but he is now dead.

About the house tower many trees. A grove of pecans sprawls in
the back. Stately cedars and huge oaks with fearsome limbs domi-
nate the front. Their aesthetic appeal is unrivaled save for the
majesty of a tall, resplendent, dense-green, and leaning magnolia,
whose blossoms in June are the color of creamy satin. The meady
aroma of its luxuriant petals perfumes the property's air.

The white, two-story, frame structure still supports the original
banistered porch that protects the home's enormous front door and
its mini-windowed vestibule. One shutter is missing from a front-
bedroom window upstairs; otherwise, the house appears much as
it must have looked when completed in the late 1830's.

Yes, that seems like a long time ago. But in DeWitt, the present is
but a tenuous advance upon the past. Perhaps that is the single
factor that gives this story its impetus or *raison d'être*.

In 1919, when Hattie married Grandall Hawthorn—then a resident engineer of South Carolina's fledgling department of highways—
and he brought her home to the Lila Grey House, the first person
she met was Jay. Jay was a black boy of seventeen, of medium
height, stoop-shouldered, with a chin that seemed just a little too
large for his face. But the whites of his eyes contrasted gently with
the light chocolate color of his skin, endowing him with a cheerful
and pleasant appearance.

Hattie smiled. "Hello, Jay," she said.

"I fine, Miz Haw'tho'n," he replied. "Mistuh Hawtho'n say he was bringin' you hahme."

"Jay's a good man," said Grandall. "There's very little Jay can't do."

The boy beamed with immense satisfaction. "I mainlees likes outside wo'k," he uttered. "Yawd wo'k, ma'am. Dass what I likes bess."

"Then I would say there's ample for you to do," laughed Hattie. "But I bet you're good with a broom too," she teased. "And a mop!"

Jay's eyes blinked, but she could see he was determined not to lose his composure. "Yass-am," he drawled. "I s'pouse I kin do dass as well."

And he could. There was very little Jay couldn't do.

One summer evening, after dinner, when Hattie and Grandall were sitting on the back screened-in porch, and Jay had retired to the small wooden cabin he occupied near the edge of the pecan grove, Hattie asked Grandall: "Grandy, tell me about Jay. However did you find him? What keeps him here? A young boy of his energy, even for a darkey, surely has a brighter future than we can offer him. . . . Though I should hate to lose him," she added.

"I know," replied Grandall. "That's true." Then he got up, mumbled something inaudible to himself, and walked out into the yard.

Hattie could not fathom why her question had brought such a response. But they had been married two years, and she had learned by now that whenever she confronted Grandall with a matter he did not wish to discuss he either answered, "I know," or grew quiet and said nothing. Often as not, as he had just done, he wandered off to another part of the house, or walked up town, or out into the yard. She knew, however, that in time he would tell her, for Grandall was not the type to conceal anything once she had inquired about it.

Several weeks later, just before dusk, as they were strolling in the front yard under one of the great cedars, Grandall said, "Hattie, not many people know this, but I got Jay from the chain gang."

"Oh my lands!" exclaimed Hattie. "Is he a convict?"

"Well, yes, sort of," he equivocated.

"Sort of?" queried Hattie. "Either he is or isn't, Grandy. Is he dangerous?" she asked.

"Hardly!" he replied. "You needn't worry."

"Poor Jay! What did he do?" she asked. "What happened?"

"It's a long story," said Grandall. "Let me try to explain. Several years ago, the county supervisor—he and I attended the university together—arranged for Jay to be placed in my custody."

"Well, I never . . .," interrupted Hattie.

"I know," Grandall stopped her, "but let me explain. You see, Jay was born near Calhoun Falls. One night, as a boy, he was caught stealing a litter of pigs from his mother's bossman, but, owing to fright, ran when the sheriff's deputies came to arrest him. When they finally captured him, he fought back, thus only compounding the charges against him. He was sentenced to twenty years at hard labor and assigned to the chain gang under the county supervisor's office. He was scarcely fourteen at the time.

"About five years ago, when we repaired the road from Green-wood to Abbeville, Jay was one of the 'convicts' on the gang. At the time, I was in charge of the project.

"Poor Jay," paused Grandall. "He stood out like a sore thumb. Young, awkward, glistening with sweat, with the face of a frightened boy! Yet he worked as hard as any two men on that gang."

"I bet he did," offered Hattie.

"In the evening, when they legged them all up, I couldn't help but feel sorry for him. Then one blistering, hot morning, a guard, for no reason I could tell, suddenly struck Jay from behind with the butt of his gun.

"He caught him right in the small of his back. The blow knocked Jay onto the hard ground, covering his hands and face gray with dust. A skinned place on his face ran with blood."

"Oh no!" flinched Hattie.

"Yes," replied Grandall. "The boy gritted his teeth but couldn't get up. The guard cursed him and made the two convicts on either side prop Jay up in the ditch and drag him along as they worked.

"The next morning when Jay was not in the gang that got out of the wagon, I inquired as to his whereabouts. The overseer, a huge man who puffed on one cigar after another, was vexed that I asked but assured me that the boy was all right.

"When three days later Jay had still not returned, I asked again. I threatened to complain to the supervisor or appeal to Columbia, if necessary."

"Good for you," said Hattie.

"The overseer puffed on his cigar and told me not to be so 'antsie.'

'He's recovernin' right now,' he said. 'Twon't be no time, he'll be right back.'

" ' 'Exactly, where is he?' I asked. 'Well, now,' said the overseer, 'if you must know, he's chained to his bunk.' "

"Oh, good heavens!" groaned Hattie.

"Yes," replied Grandall. "I asked what medical attention he had received. 'None,' said the overseer. 'Don't need none.' Then he pointed the wet end of his cigar at me. 'Now you git out of my way,' he cried, 'fore I tell the su-puh-visuh about you.' "

"What insolence!" charged Hattie.

"Agreed!" said Grandall. "Some of the white convicts had stopped work and were grinning. The black men looked up, sullen and grim. I knew I would have to report the matter.

" 'Git own back to work!' shouted the overseer. Then he turned and, swearing under his breath, glared at me, 'You know we can't let up on these nigguhs!' His face was sweating. After a moment of silence he added, 'I do 'pologize, sir.' Then he spat on the ground and walked off."

"What did you do?" asked Hattie.

"Well, it so happened," said Grandall, "that that very afternoon our supervisor had scheduled a meeting. And to my delight, several state officials were present as well as the state's director of the convict lease system. As soon as it was feasible, I explained the incident to them. I didn't even know Jay's name at the time, but I implored them to investigate the matter and offered to make the boy my ward, if that were in any way possible.

"The supervisor said he liked the idea, but didn't know. The director of the convict lease system advised caution.

"To make a long story short, after much prompting and repeated appeals on my part, the supervisor finally arranged to have Jay assigned to my custody and to have him transferred to any location I saw fit. I should then be responsible for him until such time as he completed his full sentence, which won't be for another fourteen years."

"Gracious!" exclaimed Hattie. "What's to happen then?"

"He's to be free."

Hattie's face filled with distress. "How horrible to think that the Lila Grey House is his prison and we his wardens! Oh, I wish you hadn't told me."

Grandall took her hand and kissed it. "Sooner or later you had to know," he said. "Things will work out."

"What if he should run away?"

"He won't," replied Grandall. "Jay understands."

"Oh, I do hope so," sighed Hattie.

Many springs came and passed, the tall jonquils bloomed in their beds, the magnolia blossoms scented the air with their sweet nectar, autumn winds rattled the dried leaves under the great trees, and successive Novembers brought the harvesting of pecans. Then one April afternoon, some nine years later, Hattie and Jay were walking up town when the following incident occurred.

It was during the Depression and two impoverished men were standing on the sidewalk in front of the hotel. Jay, as he always did, followed Hattie at a respectable distance. He was pushing an empty wheelbarrow which Hattie intended to fill with two, one-hundred-pound sacks of fertilizer at the hardware. Ordinarily, she would have sent Jay by himself, but it was such a beautiful day that she wanted to get outside herself. Besides, W. D. Stone stocked his hardware with everything from fresh eggs to mousetraps and tractor parts to harnesses. And even if money were tight, it would be a joy to look around. Times were so depressing, as the soiled and crumpled clothes on the two men testified.

As she passed the largest of the two—the one chewing on the slimy butt of an unlit cigar—the terrible premonition crept over her that she had met him before. Where? When? She could not tell.

Hard times had etched its disparaging marks on many men, but she was confident this man's slovenly was inveterate. When he smiled at her, she shuddered inwardly. She scarcely noticed the second.

She had passed them and was about to wave to Reverend Grail, the A.R.P. pastor, a proud Virginian by birth, who was examining tomato plants on the sidewalk in front of the hardware, when the man chewing on the unlit cigar butt elbowed his companion. "Well, well, would you look at that," he chuckled.

Her heart climbed in her throat. She could hear Jay stop.

"Hey, boy!" taunted the second man. "Don't you know yo' place?"

The big man laughed. "Where's you' chains, boy?" he spat.

Hattie thought she would faint. She knew instantly who they were. She could see Reverend Grail look up. Mrs. Grail and Mr. Stone had just stepped out of the hardware. W. D.'s little son was with him.

At that same moment, she heard Jay let out a desperate grunt and, as she turned, saw him drive the wheelbarrow forcibly into the two men. The fatter man collapsed in it with a heavy thump. A look of terror filled Jay's face. Then he turned and ran across the street, disappearing into the hedges along the barber shop.

In a daze, Hattie glanced down. Where the large man's head had struck the wheelbarrow, blood glistened in the sunlight. He had rolled onto the ground and was attempting to pull himself up. Bright blood oozed from an ugly gash on his nose. Even his cigar butt was smeared with blood. Her esophagus suddenly felt hot. "Oh," moaned Hattie as she fainted in the arms of Reverend Grail.

As she came to, she faintly recognized Mrs. Grail's voice. As she opened her eyes, she realized she was lying on a musty sofa. At first, she could not imagine her whereabouts, but gradually it occurred to her that she must be in the dingy lobby of the hotel.

Mrs. Grail was patting her face with a damp, perfumed handkerchief. "She's coming to," said Mrs. Grail. "Thank heavens, Raymond, she's coming to."

The Reverend Grail looked very worried. "Ah you all right, Mrs. Haw-thawn?" he asked in his broad Virginia accent.

"Yes," answered Hattie, fully conscious now. "But Jay! Where's Jay?"

"Vanished!" replied Reverend Grail. "Mis-tuh Jay is gawn!"

Hattie could not help but smile at Reverend Grail's reference to Jay as "Mis-tuh Jay." He had always called him that as a matter of politeness. But when she glanced to her right and saw Jay's former overseer sitting in the doorway, pressing a wadded towel to his bloody face, the horror and uncertainty of what had happened seized her with new fright.

"Poor Jay," she groaned. "The boy's innocent. Innocent!" she asserted.

"Now, now," calmed Mrs. Grail. "Don't be upset. These gentlemen have explained. . . ."

"Ohh," sighed Hattie, "that can't be. They'll only take him back to jail."

"No, no," comforted Reverend Grail. "I hawdly think so."

Hattie closed her eyes, then reopened them. Mr. Stone was peering over Mrs. Grail's shoulder. His spectacles had slipped down

54

his nose, but she welcomed the words he spoke.

"Hattie," he intoned, "don't you worry yourself about Jay. Some of us have known all along. Grandall couldn't keep that kind of secret forever. Besides, DeWitt's too small a town for that. We'll fetch him back. You just rest now."

"That's right," said Mrs. Grail. "Raymond and I will help you home."

"Yes," drawled the pastor. "We'll think of a way to retrieve Mis-tuh Jay."

Hattie breathed a sigh of relief, at least momentarily.

The retrieving of Jay proved far more difficult than anyone had thought. Grandall paced the halls of the Lila Grey House for many evenings, as if Jay's flight were the exile of an only son. It was mainly through the labors of Reverend Grail, who managed to convince the pastor of the nearby, black, Zion A.M.E. church that absolutely nothing would happen to Jay if he returned that, at long last, one July morning, Jay showed up at the back door. His clothing was tattered and dusty, and both his shoes were missing.

Hattie was later embarrassed when she retold the incident, for the first thing she remembered saying to him in a scolding voice was, "Jay, where are your shoes?"

"I'z has gib dem to a po fambly," he replied. "Da one dass he'ped me da mos'. But I'z hahme now," he grinned.

"Oh, Jay!" she burst with delight. "Thank God you're back!"

"Yass-am," he allowed.

The remaining five years of Jay's sentence slipped away all too quickly for Hattie. She had often rehearsed the coming scene, but she never imagined it would end as it did. At times she had pictured Jay standing on the back screened-in porch, Grandall having confirmed his release, and hearing him say with droll gravity, "Yass-suh, Mis-tuh Haw-tho'n, I knows, suh. But I'z wan' ta stay h'ar. Pleeze let me stay." At other times she would envision him packing his paltry belongings in a cloth valise and slipping away in the night.

It worried her how it would end. They could always pay him wages, but hardly what he was worth. Besides, hadn't they deprived him of enough of his life already? How dear a price to pay for a litter of pigs! It brought tears to her eyes when she actually thought about it. Sometimes it frightened her and filled her with guilt. "O God," she would pray to herself, "he must have done something worse than

55

that? Surely he had to!"

When the day of his release arrived, Grandall called Jay into his study. Hattie stood beside her husband, as they had agreed. Jay came in, smiling more than she thought he should, but gracious as only Jay could be.

"I's beholdin'," he said. "Y'all an' dis Li-La Gray House has show been my haben. Old Jay done say to his-self manny times, 'Jay, you be dead now—dead on dat chain gan', sabe fo' Mis-tuh Haw-tho'n an' dis Li'La Grey Houze!' Dass fo' show!"

Hattie was deeply moved. How she hoped he would ask to stay on. Grandall handed him the envelope with the two fifty-dollar bills they had agreed to give him.

"Go on," said Grandall. "Look inside."

Jay did. "Woo-wee!" he exclaimed. "My wibe show be glad to see dem. An' my little uns, too!"

"You're married?" asked Hattie. "You mean all this time you've been married? Jay, why didn't you tell us?"

"I 'fraid, ma'am. Yass-am, I wuz."

Grandall laughed. "I don't believe it."

"Yass-suh, 'tis so. Dat time I run off. I married da girl what hide me, down in Antra-ville. Sometime on Sahndee, when you ain't seen me 'round, dass where I's been. I's leabe here late a Saddee night and gits back 'fo' y'all knowed it. Done got two chilluns," he grinned.

"Jay, I don't know what to say," cried Hattie.

"Yass-am," he smiled. Then his face saddened as he looked toward the door. "I reckon I be j'inin' my fambly, now," he said. He looked at both of them with his big gentle eyes.

Hattie's own began to fill with tears.

"Good-bye," said Grandall, extending Jay his hand.

"Yass-suh," replied Jay, shaking it somberly. "May de good God bless you."

Now one might think that this is the *terminus ad quem* of the story, but that's not how it ended. For the next five years or so, Grandall and Hattie would occasionally see Jay and his family, sometimes in Antreville, at times in DeWitt, at other times in Abbeville. Then, with the coming of the war, he left the county, and no one seemed to know where he moved.

Thirty more years came and passed. During that time Grandall died, and toward the end of it Hattie turned eighty. Late, one warm, fall afternoon, in our own decade, Hattie was picking up small limbs that had blown down in the yard and was trying to rake up magnolia leaves, when a rusty pickup truck drove slowly by the house and stopped near the end of the property. The door on the passenger's side creaked open, and, after some delay, an elderly colored man struggled out. His hair was the color of dirty cotton, and his frame sagged with age. He clutched a cane in one hand, and a grocery bag was tucked under his other arm. He motioned to the driver, and the truck moved away.

Hattie stared at the massive, stooped shoulders and, as the old man came closer, studied his chin. "Jay," she whispered to herself. "Why it can't be! Mis-tuh Jay, is that you?" she asked aloud.

"Yess-am," he smiled. "Haz you had a good day, Miz Haw'tho'n?"

"Oh, Jay, it is good to see you!"

"Dass is a feelin' of mu-chu-ality," he added respectfully.

"Well, where have you been?" she demanded.

"My wibe is dead," he said. "My sahns is tu'ned out bad. I'z all wo'ned out. An' I ain't got no hahme but dis Li-La Grey House. I can still ten' dis yawd, if you jus' gibe dis ol' body a chance."

And so Mis-tuh Jay came home. He outlived Hattie by two years. Her will provided for his keep until his death. Afterwards, the house and its grounds passed, as a deferred gift, into the hands of the A.R.P. college at DeWitt, known as Ebenezer College.

Sometimes when the March air is warm, and I have a moment to spare, I slip out of the hardware and walk down to the Lila Grey House. I love to pace slowly along the sidewalk and stare at those wide beds of jonquils, awash in colorful bloom. Sometimes I just gaze at the house, or across the yard at its tall, sad hedges, and listen to the wind rustle the magnolia leaves.

# THE HOUSE
# ON
# CALHOUN
# STREET

# The House on Calhoun Street

On the corner of Main and Calhoun streets, set back among diseased and dying oaks, squats a single story uncared-for house. Its roof sports many gables, and its faded green shingles are thin and crumpled along the eaves. The putty-colored frame house badly needs a coat of paint. A long sagging porch darkens its doorway.

No shutters decorate this forgotten lodgment's windows. No flower boxes redeem its rotting sills. No telephone lines connect it with the busy and friendly commerce of community life. The electrical wires leading into the house sag in a visible state of deterioration.

The house itself rests on crumbling brick pillars, whose dry mortar has cracked and fallen off in spindly pieces. No underpinning protects the exposed beams of the floor.

The house cannot be said to have a yard. Here and there tufts of grass and red-speckled mushrooms sprout up around the roots of the dying trees. The ground itself is damp and bare. From Calhoun Street, the yard appears as dark as the rotting timbers under the front porch.

Tall grass and weeds, wild plum and honeysuckle, grow in profusion behind the house. The pines, at the rear end of the lot, have been enveloped by dense streamers of kudzu. A small tricycle rusts near the heavy vines. A child's swing set and the T-bars of an old clothesline bulge barely visible under the canopy of tendrils.

Hardly a dwelling place fit for habitation, this dreary house has been the home of many a transient family that has come and gone in DeWitt. Within one year, no less than five different families occupied its rooms.

Observer to it all, and sadly touched by the human passage that made its way to this house, was a young English professor at Ebenezer College. If not daily, at least often each week, he noted the state of the human condition that this depressing house quartered.

He lived in a new air-conditioned apartment opposite the dwelling. His upstairs bedroom window provided a direct view of its front yard and moldering porch, making him privy to the secrets upon its stage.

The house was vacant the first spring he moved into the apartment. On rainy days he watched the rain stream off its eaves and oveflow the rusted guttering along the porch. He assumed the old house would soon be razed.

It came as something of a shock when, returning from the opening session of his summer school course, he heard the laughter of small children on the porch. He looked across the street to behold three, staring, pre-school-aged children—all little girls.

Only the oldest child wore shoes. The smaller ones were barefooted. All their dresses were faded and worn and looked worse than hand-me-downs from the shabbiest sort of rag barrel.

The oldest child smiled, cautiously raised her hand, and waved to him. Immediately, her younger sister waved, too. The tiniest girl cried in a loud, sweet voice, "Hi, Hi!" Her middle sister joined her. "Hi mister! Hi mister man!"

He waved in reply. "Hi to you, too," he called. He could not help but mark that, in spite of their rags, they were beautiful children.

Suddenly, a large, haggard woman appeared at the screen door. She jerked it open and descended angrily upon the girls.

"Hush up!" she lashed at them. "I don't want to hear no more talk like that! Do you hear?"

She stepped out onto the porch and motioned for them to get into the house, instantly. The littlest girl began to cry. Her loud sobs were filled with protest and fear of the woman's rage.

As the children filed into the house, the woman said for the professor to hear, "How many times have I told you not to wave at strangers? Don't you ever wave at that man again!"

The screen door slammed, and the children were shoved into the gloom of the house.

After that, whenever the professor saw the little girls, he never quite knew how to act. Still he looked their way and smiled. The children would stop playing, stand in silence, and look longingly at him. How he wanted to wave and hear the littlest one belt out her greeting!

It concerned him that the woman rarely came out of the house.

She drove an old dilapidated green Chevrolet, which she parked near the end of the porch. The only time she seemed to use it was when she went to buy groceries or do the laundry. None of the children could open the Chevy's heavy doors, and she would scold them for being so useless.

If the woman had a husband, or the children a father, the man never came to gladden their darkness. The young professor wondered how they managed to survive.

As the weeks dragged into August, and the hot nights became unbearable, the woman moved several chairs out onto the porch. There the children played, while she fussed, until the night air grew less sufferable and they could go back inside.

Frequently, he would turn out his light, raise his window slightly, and eavesdrop on their din. To his amazement, the woman would hold the littlest girl on her lap and hum. When he went to bed, such scenes tugged on his heart, long into the night.

One Friday, he resolved he would not go to "Yoder's" that night for dinner, or later drive to Anderson for a movie. Instead, he would drive to Abbeville and buy those little girls each a dress and a doll.

He felt good thinking about it all morning. He could hardly wait until he was free. He hurried home, ate a late lunch, then drove to Abbeville. He parked his car by the square, near the Confederate monument, and walked briskly toward the largest department store.

On his way back to DeWitt, he savored the reception he would receive. He would go up to the door, introduce himself, and insist that the mother accept the dresses for the girls. Then he would hand each child her doll.

When he returned, he was surprised to see a shiny blue Toyota in the yard. A well-dressed man with a beige shirt and brown tie was coming out of the house. The green Chevy was gone. So were the children.

The professor parked his car and stepped out. The man called to him. "Hey, fellow! You haven't seen the woman who was staying here, have you?"

Come to think of it, he hadn't. Not for several days in fact. "No!" he said with alarm. "What's happened?"

The man cursed. "Renters! Ran off!" he said. "They owed us for two months. Should have known she would never pay."

He slammed the front door and locked it. "At least they won't get back in," he said. "Changed the lock on them!" he laughed. He walked to his car and drove off.

The young professor was dumbfounded. Not knowing what to do, he got back into his car and stared across the street at the lonely porch. He laid his hand on the package of dresses and dolls and just sat there long into the evening.

When by the middle of the next week the woman and the children had not returned, he knew they were gone forever.

The remaining weeks of August slipped by uneventfully. Save for the oppressive heat and the stifling nights, the house on Calhoun Street resumed its moldering, empty appearance.

At least the children were not there to suffer the heat. But where were they? he wondered.

He scarcely noted the couple that moved in next. They occupied the house about the middle of September. They had two children—teenagers—and drove a late model pickup truck.

The rough-looking, lanky, blue-jeaned father left the house each morning about seven and returned about four in the afternoon. His clothing was always streaked with grease. So were his hands and face.

One free Wednesday afternoon, while on his way to Anderson, the professor recognized the man alongside the road. He was working on a piece of heavy equipment, being assembled in the dirt yard of a tool shop near Belton. The yard was potted with mud holes and oil spills and strewn with radiators and truck parts. He waved to his neighbor, but the man never looked up.

Toward the end of October, this couple, too, was gone. The professor realized it one weekend when it occurred to him that he had not seen the truck in several days. Now all was silent again.

Frost killed the kudzu in the back lot, leaving the pines mantled in a net of muddy gray. In the front yard, and along the sides of the house, the oak trees slowly dropped their reddish-brown leaves. The professor watched them pile up in the folds of the roof and clog the rusted gutters.

Just before Thanksgiving, a threesome of hippies moved in. Their leader appeared to be a stout, stringy-haired girl. One of her male companions was as hefty as she and wore a red bandanna around his forehead. The other man was short with a thick, black, crop of beard. All three dressed in denim pants and jackets. The men wore boots;

the girl went barefooted.

They drove a flashy blue van with electric colors vibrating out from a red and yellow, Yin-Yang symbol, painted on the left panel.

In spite of their appearance, they were quiet, stayed mostly in the house, and received no visitors. By January, they, too, were gone.

An ice storm finally brought the guttering off the front porch. It fell in half-a-dozen rusted pieces, spraying decayed leaves across the icy ground. Some days later the man in the blue Toyota came by. He checked the lock and kicked the debris under the porch.

Toward early February, an elderly woman, confined to a wheelchair, was brought to the house. One man helped her from the back seat of a Mercury sedan while another steadied the wheelchair. Then they picked up both her and the wheelchair, carried her to the house, and lifted her up on the porch. The professor could see that all of this was against her will.

The older and balder of the two men unlocked the door and pushed her inside. She appeared to be crying. The younger man had gone back to the car for a suitcase.

They left soon afterward but returned later in the evening with boxes of groceries and what appeared to be personal things.

When they were about to depart, the woman wheeled herself out onto the porch and openly wept in their presence. The two men looked awkward and miserable. They left her sitting there in the cold.

The pastor of the DeWitt Baptist Church called on her the following afternoon. Thereafter, the professor noted, either the pastor or members of his church visited her as often as possible. Six weeks later he noticed the house was empty again.

More than ever now, the house depressed him. He hated to look out upon it from his window. He wondered how many years would have to pass before he could forget the faces of those little girls.

The sunshine of March brought warmth and light to the corner again. Once more the dying oaks put forth new leaves, though paler and fewer in number. Grass struggled to grow in the front yard and jonquils bloomed on the east side of the house. The old crumbling home evoked both nostalgia and anger from him.

For the first time in a long while he realized how sheltered his own life had been. He wondered how many sad and luckless families occupied still sadder and more cheerless dwellings than this hulk on Calhoun Street.

A great wave of depression rose up out of the sea of his troubled thoughts and crashed restlessly upon his conscience. "What can be done?" he mumbled. "Won't it always be this way?"

That night he had trouble gathering the usual solace from his favorite English and American poets or finding security in the familiar caves of philosophical retreat.

Several weeks later, it came to him as something of a personal alarm when he realized the house was being rented yet a fifth time.

"Not again!" he muttered, as he watched its new occupant slip out of her VW and slowly survey the moldering home.

To his surprise, she was young, alone, comely to behold; indeed, beautiful. "My word!" he exclaimed, "she can't be going there! There must be some mistake."

He felt instant love and pity for her. He threw down a book he was reading, descended the stairs, and hurried out into the street.

"Hello!" he called, as he came up through the dank yard and the mushrooms. "I'm Dean Emerson. A professor at Ebenezer. Are you moving in?" he asked.

She looked at him uneasily, but smiled. "Yes," she replied, not quite knowing what else to say.

"I thought I might be of some assistance, if you are," he offered.

She smiled again. "You're kind to offer, but the movers will be here tomorrow."

She cautiously shook hands with him. "I'm Angela Reid," she said.

How beautiful she was! There was a strength about her he admired. There was a trace of sadness, however, in her eyes. He guessed her to be his own age, 31.

"I do have things to do," she said politely.

"I understand," he replied. "I just wanted to welcome you to DeWitt."

"Thank you," she said.

He was not there when the van brought her furniture—what few things she had—but he was pleased to hear a Chopin piece emanating aesthetically from the living room, filling the spring air with its romantic notes. How technically purely the piece was being performed! He wondered what recording company had released it.

That weekend he went to the mountains to visit friends. Upon his return Sunday evening, he was surprised to read in the paper where a Mrs. Angela Reid of DeWitt, corner of Main and Calhoun, was advertising piano lessons. "A 'Mrs.'!" he said with despair. "It can't be!"

The next evening he went to her door, knocked, and, when she opened it, announced his intention to take lessons. She laughed but agreed to work with him and scheduled their first meeting.

By June, the lessons had brought them closer together. And little by little he began to learn the secrets of her life.

He learned that her husband, a Viet Nam veteran, was dead. He learned that she had been in a hospital, recovering for some time. He learned that she was from Georgia, a graduate of Agnes Scott.

He learned of her father's bankruptcy, her parents' deaths, all coming about the time of her husband's. He sensed there was something more, something deep, painful, tormenting, something she couldn't yet talk about.

From time to time, for periods of two days, she would strangely disappear. Upon her return, however, she would seem more radiant, buoyant, and lovely than ever.

They began to date, and soon their love for each other flowered into courtship and the imminence of marriage. Finally, one evening, while sitting together on the piano bench, she suddenly turned, put her arms around his neck, and began to cry.

"There is something you must know," she said. "I can't keep it a secret from you any longer."

"Please tell me," he answered, fearing at last this moment, now that it came.

"I had children by my former marriage. They were taken from me when I had to be hospitalized. They were placed in the custody of my husband's aunt."

The professor felt deep embarrassment and sorrow for her and listened with love.

"At first, all went well. But the government checks got misplaced, and she and the children began running out of money. Besides, she's a poor woman, an uneducated and rather tragic figure herself, and didn't know what to do. I was in the hospital and wasn't even informed."

Suddenly, an intense pain griped his heart. He thought of the little girls. Surely, it couldn't be!

"For a year and a half, she lived here and there, just anywhere she could find lodging, and fed the children and herself on the mea-gerest of rations."

He sat up, erect. "Are the children little girls?" he demanded.

"Yes!" she said, with surprise. "Three!"

"Where are they?" he asked, with a groan.

"In Columbia. In a home. I go to see them twice a month. I want to bring them back, but I must first prove to the state that I'm accountable and stable and a worthy mother."

He ground his teeth and fought back his tears.

"I know you won't want me now," she cried softly. "We'd only complicate your life."

"Complicate!" he shouted. "No, no! Fulfill!" he laughed, as he gripped her in his tight embrace, searchingly gathering unto himself the three little girls, whose dresses and dolls were still gift-wrapped in the floor of his closet and whose voices, from that first summer's day, cried to him from the secret-most places of his heart.

# A LIGHT
# IN THE FOREST

# A Light In The Forest

Big George had hunted bear most of his life. Only there were no more bear to hunt along the Savannah. After the bear were gone, he tracked deer.

His favorite section of the river was the stretch just below the long, rusted bridge west of Iva to several miles south of Calhoun Falls. He loved to hunt along its banks, hop out onto its great ribs of outcroppings, and listen to the sun-sparkled water swirl and eddy by.

When the river was up and the water ran high, he would climb into a tree, listen to the mighty river groan, and watch its muddy waves leap the long outcroppings of rock.

It saddened him to know that one day even this section of the river would be gone. For once the Russell Dam was completed near Calhoun Falls, this stretch he loved would exist no more.

Sometimes in the summer, when the river was low, he would take a long pole and vault from outcropping to outcropping, as far as he could down river. Then he would kneel down on one of the rocks, cup his fingers in the water, and stare down the wild furrows of the river. How he loved to watch it slip between the outcroppings and ripple the long, muddy tendrils of river weed and moss!

George missed the bear. He missed the excitement of finding their paw prints in the soft mud along the river and of tracking them deep into the woods.

Now the largest prints he found were those of wild dogs. Sometimes it frightened him to find as many as he did. No wonder the deer were spooky and so difficult to stalk.

One cold winter morning, while hunting along the river, he discovered a child's footprints in the gravelly sand. The child was barefooted, and its small tracks left clear impressions in the cold earth.

The poor child! thought George. For the tracks were fresh, the air chilling to the bone, and a light mist drifted over the river, darkening the woods.

With curiosity, he followed the footprints about thirty yards, where he discovered the convergence of dog tracks upon the child's. "I must hurry," he grunted aloud.

He carried a twelve-gauge, double-barrelled shotgun, loaded with buckshot, and wore a .32 caliber pistol on his hip. Thank heavens he had brought his pistol! he thought.

Once he entered the woods, every tracking instinct George had acquired and every resource he had learned flowed to his help. He moved quickly and easily through the woods, but the trail was difficult to follow in the mist and cold.

He lost it momentarily in a thicket of spiny pin oaks. The sharp barbs on the dense lower branches tore a hole in his jacket and gashed his hands and face. He knew the child could not have come this way.

Finally, he stumbled out upon a path and discovered the tracks again. The small, unhurried steps indicated that the child was unaware that it was being followed.

George ran along the path until it seemed to disappear. Then he bent down to examine the trail.

Suddenly, he sensed he was not alone. Every instinct warned him that he was being watched. He eased the safety off his shotgun and listened.

The woods were dark and silent. Without moving his head, he glanced to the right, then to the left. Quietly, quickly, and thoughtfully, he stood erect. He braced his back against a tree.

He eased his right hand to his hip and unsnapped his holster. Just as he did, a large black dog lunged at his throat. It seemed to come out of nowhere! If his back had not been against the tree, he would have fallen under the animal's heavy weight. He swung his shotgun upwards and killed the dog at point-blank range.

He saw a second dog crouch to spring. It was a huge, ugly, German shepherd. Its fangs were bared, its gums bright red, and its lips curled and quivering. He blew its skull off just as it leaped, but he stumbled in the process and fell down.

As the rest of the pack closed in, he fired into the yelping moil of fangs and fur until his pistol was empty. If it had not been for his padded hunting jacket, he would have been ripped to pieces.

It was over in an instant. Five dogs lay dead. But he was visibly shaken. He could not control his trembling. For a moment, he thought he would vomit.

Finally, he stood up, let out a loud yell, flailed his arms back and forth, and took several deep breaths to release his tension. The trembling stopped.

He felt his arms, face, legs, and hands. Miraculously, he had not been bitten. He retrieved his shotgun and surveyed the carnage of blood-smeared fur and bone.

The mist was beginning to lift. With it his bewilderment passed, and he suddenly remembered the child. Where might it be? Could it be dead? Had he surprised the pack before it had caught up with the child?

He was about to renew his search for the tracks when he heard the crunch of a branch ahead in the woods. He crouched, uncertain what to expect. He heard a second crunch, then a third.

To his surprise, less than twenty yards away, a gaunt old Negro, cradling a long-barelled shotgun of ancient vintage in his arms, was stealing his way toward him.

Behind the Negro stumbled a frightened little girl. She was clad in a torn dress, an old army sweater, and a brown stocking cap.

The Negro had already spotted George. He raised his hand and smiled. "Hot diggity!" he grinned. "You sho' got 'em dead! What a bless-ed de-livererance! Um! That is so! Are you hu't?"

"No, I'm fine!" replied George, as he got to his feet, relieved to see the child and charmed by the old Negro. He could see that the child was almost white.

"I was hunting by the river," George nodded in its direction, "when I saw the little girl's footprints. About that time I saw the dogs' too. I feared the worst."

"Well, they been after us fo' weeks," said the Negro. "Then, day 'fo' yes-tuh-day, they up an' disappeared. 'Janie,' I said, 'they gone away! Go down to the river an' see if you can't fin' dem shoes you lost.' It is so cold! An' I ain't even got no socks fo' her. No, sir!"

George looked down at the little girl's feet. She was no longer barefooted but was wearing a tattered pair of army mittens on her feet.

George glanced toward the old man's. His heels and ankles were white with dried mud. His bare feet were thrust into a cracked and flaking pair of heelless and untied shoes.

"I'm sorry I didn't see her shoes," said George. "I'll be glad to help you look for them."

"No use now!" allowed the old Negro. "River done got 'em! 'Sides, we got us a fire in de cabin, an' that keeps us plen'ty warm," he grinned.

"Won't you come an' join us?" he offered. "Come on up to de cabin! We owes it to you. God knows, you has come like a Savior! Ain't that so, Janie?"

The little girl clasped the old man's overalls, swung around his leg, and snickered. "Uh-huh!" she smiled, as she looked up at George.

George felt embarrassed to receive such praise. But he was moved with love and pity at the sight of the little girl.

To be candid, he did not want to go. But when his eyes met with Janie's, a voice in his heart urged him to accept. "It will be my pleasure," he smiled.

George offered the little girl his hand. She held it tight. Then he followed the two toward a path and a distant light in the forest.

As they approached a clearing, George saw that the light was a smoldering fire under a black iron kettle. Nearby, on the edge of the clearing, leaned an old shed—their cabin. A piece of tarpaulin served as its door.

The old man pulled it to one side. "Please go in," he motioned.

George stepped inside onto a dirt floor. A bed springs, piled with blankets and a filthy quilt, was pushed up against one wall. Several old crates served as tables. Some stood upright and were stuffed with clothes.

Smoke drifted in the air. Coals glowed on an open hearth, surrounded by large rocks. A hole in the ceiling served as a vent. Janie squirmed by George and hurried to the hearth to warm herself.

"Please sit on the springs," pointed the old Negro. "You' the fu'st white man ev-uh to visit our lodgment," he smiled proudly.

George sat down.

The Negro pulled up one of the crates and sat on it. "I know whut you're thinkin'." he said. He put his arm around Janie, and she climbed up into his lap. He ran his long black fingers over her stubby hair. His eyes filled with tears.

"I know whut I done was wrong," he began, "but I din't know whut

74

else to do. Five yea's ago, a gang o' white boys raped my only baby daught-uh. She died givin' birth to Janie. Me an' my wife cared fo' the baby fo' two yea's. Then Tululu died. I din't know whut to do.

"Some of the brothern and sistern say that the State was gonna come an' take Janie away, that they won't gonna let no old black man keep such a fair-skinned child to hisself. So I run away. I up an' left where I was an' come here.

"I can't tell you who I am or where I'm from. That ain't fo' you to know. But that's how we come here. There's a family back over the hill that helps us some. But I ain't gonna let nobody take my baby from me. No, suh!" he hummed, as he wrapped his arms about the child.

"I understand," replied George. "She's a lovely child." He smiled at Janie. "If you were mine, honey, I wouldn't let *nobody* have you either."

George and the old man talked on. Then George rose, thanked the old Negro for his hospitality, picked Janie up in his arms, clung to her smile for a moment, returned her to her grandfather, and said goodbye.

When George reached the river and saw the child's footprints again, he stopped. He knelt beside two of the tiny tracks and measured them with his hand.

When he had completed the measurements, he stood up and surveyed the area. He noted every detail of the river, its east bank, and the woods.

An hour elapsed before he reached his pickup truck near the bridge, west of Calhoun Falls. But minutes later he parked it beside the small shopping center in town.

He bought Janie a pair of shoes and her grandfather a pair of boots. He also purchased some clothing and a warm, bright-colored blanket. He had to charge it all, but his credit was good.

He drove to the grocery store and bought some staples and food items he thought would keep. He included in the bags some chewing tobacco, a package of candy, a child's toothbrush, and a tube of toothpaste.

Early the next morning, he drove back to the bridge, parked his truck in the pull-off area, locked it, and packed the goods he had bought down to the river. He retrieved his steps of yesterday to the gravelly bank where he had found the child's tracks.

He picked up the trail without effort and followed it into the woods. He was relieved when he smelled the smoke of their fire and saw the cabin in the distance.

The old Negro was quite taken by surprise. "May God bless you!" he whispered, as he helped George unsling his pack.

"He has," answered George.

The little girl's eyes widened with delight when he handed her the new shoes.

When George returned home that evening, the old man and the little girl accompanied him as far as the river. After he waved goodbye to them, he wept openly on his way back to the bridge.

George had never been married. He had never had a family. He had filled most of his life with hunting and fishing, with hiking and being alone. Now, for a reason he could not explain, he no longer wanted to be alone.

Thereafter, at least once a week that winter, George returned to their cabin. He never missed a Saturday. Sometimes Janie and "Pop," as he called the old Negro now, would meet him at the river. Often, he went back on Sundays.

When spring came, George resolved that somehow he had to get Pop and Janie out of the forest. He didn't know how, but he knew he must try.

Both needed a home and medical care. Janie needed children to play with. It was time for their exile to end. But how? Pray, God, how?

George walked along the river. He hopped out onto one of its great outcroppings and listened to the water slip by. The sun's bright light dazzled his eyes when he stared into the water.

He looked up the river, away from the sun. "How?" he repeated. "Will you tell me, how? Time is even running out for you, old river," he sighed.

That spring it rained often and hard. It rained more than George had ever seen it rain in his life.

The river rose and crested above the outcroppings. Streams along the Savannah became torrents themselves. The footing was hazardous, even far back away from the bank. Water lapped into the woods everywhere. George had to make many detours to reach the cabin.

"You need to get out of here!" George said to Pop. "The river is rising! You and Janie could be swept away!"

"Not hardly," laughed Pop. "I ain't never seen the waters come back dis far. You worry too much about us already. The good Lord will take care of us."

Janie began to cry.

"Pop, I'm going to take you and Janie out of here!" said George.

"You ain't gonna do no such thing!" countered the Negro. "I ain't goin' nowhere where I might lose dis child!" He put his arms protectingly about her.

"Papa, I 'fraid!" cried Janie. "Help us, Missuh George! I 'fraid!"

"Pop, we have to go," urged George.

The old Negro looked bewildered. He looked down helplessly toward Janie, then back up at George. "Maybe we'll go with you fo' the night," he smiled, "If that pleases you and this young-un!"

Janie's face glowed with happiness. "We gonna see Missuh George's place, Papa?"

"Yes, honey," replied the old Negro. "We're gonna go, but just fo' the night!"

He turned to George. "Let me put my gun up where the water can't reach it, just in case! I also needs a few things."

"OK," said George.

George found a jacket he had bought Janie and helped her put it on. He could hear it raining harder than ever outside. Water dripped from the hole above, then ran in a stream from the ceiling, and hissed when it hit the hot ashes in the hearth.

"Get your cap on, honey," he said. "You'll need that too."

George lifted back the tarpaulin and glanced outside. Water was beginning to lap in the clearing. "Pop, we must leave now!" George said with alarm. He immediately picked Janie up in his arms.

"I'm comin'!" called Pop.

The old man had climbed up on a crate and was placing his gun on a ledge just under the roof. Suddenly, the crate collapsed. Pop fell backwards with a loud groan and struck his head against a rock beside the hearth. Janie screamed.

"Pop!" called George. "Pop, are you all right?"

The old man's head slipped off the rock, but his body did not stir. His eyes stared at the ceiling.

George held Janie in his arms and looked down at the sad, frail figure. George realized the old Negro was dead.

"Papa, Papa!" cried Janie. "I want my Papa!"

George eased her down and let her hug the old man. Then he knelt beside him, closed his eyelids, picked him up gently, and laid him on the bed springs.

"Papa's dead! Papa's dead, isn't he?" sobbbed Janie.

"Yes," replied George. "Pop is dead."

He covered him with the new blanket. Suddenly, he turned and swooped Janie up in his arms.

"Janie, I'm sorry, but we must go! We must go now! You must say goodbye to Papa and hold tight to me! Do you hear?"

"Papa, Papa!" screamed Janie.

"I love you," whispered George. "Now, hold tight to me! Whatever happens, don't let go!"

"I won't!" she sobbed. "Oh, Papa, Papa!"

George brushed the tarpaulin to one side and stepped out into the river with Janie. The water was already up to his thighs. It swirled around him and almost knocked him down. He braced himself against the cabin and pushed himself and Janie toward higher ground.

A tall cedar collapsed in front of them. It splashed into the water to their right. It fell with a sickening crunch. Its roots, however, remained lodged on the bank. A low hill rose behind it, then higher ground.

George groped for the cedar's firry limbs and pulled himself and Janie forward. Slowly, they made it to the hill.

"Look!" cried Janie.

George turned. The cabin was gone. The tall cedar had crushed it, and the debris was floating down river.

George clasped Janie in his arms. The river had given the child to him, but at the price of Pop. He listened to its awesome roar, then turned and carried the child through the rain toward higher ground.

Sometimes on sunny days, the two take walks beside the river. When the sun is bright and the river is low and the outcroppings jut above the water, the Savannah is a beautiful sight. It is truly one of America's last great rivers.

"Daddy, is this the place where you first found my footprints," asks Janie.

"Yes, sweetheart," George replies. Then he bends down and stares across the river. He squints at the sun and watches the eddies swirl around the outcroppings. He almost always thinks of the old Negro and hugs the child in his arms.

# THE
# OLD HOTEL

# The Old Hotel

The quaint two-story building that occupies a central place on the main street of DeWitt is known as "the old Hotel." From a distance, its facade reminds one of the Alamo. This is owing to the shape of its crown and the stucco exterior that has cracked in many places, patches of which have fallen off the old brick.

No one knows its precise age. A photograph from the 1880s preserves its appearance at its height of activity. In the photo, a long porch graces its front. An elaborate gingerbread molding adds to its charm. Overhead, a banistered balcony looks down placidly upon the town's broad dirt street.

Today, both the banisters and molding are gone. Dense mulberry bushes brush up against the building. Its salmon-colored brick absorbs the sun. Tall shafts of bamboo enwall its rear entrance. In the spring, festoons of wisteria drape the hotel's back porch, and sparrows build nests high up under the building's gutters.

Upstairs, on the southwest side of the hotel, windowpanes are missing, and the wind blows into the rooms, whipping tattered curtains to-and-fro. Downstairs, the shades are drawn. Along the front sidewalk, delicate patches of moss glisten in the shadows and grow in the dampness of the building's cracks.

Considering that no guests have occupied its rooms since 1941, time has been kind to the old hotel. Now, as if a shrine, it guards DeWitt's Main Street and attracts many a passing motorist's eye.

According to Samuel A. Bagly, whose history of DeWitt is housed in the archives of Ebenezer College, the hotel was built in 1852 by Charles Lefond Agnou, a Huguenot. Agnou, the town's leading mercantiler, had built it on the very site where, a hundred years earlier, an old Indian trading post had stood.

This trading post had been not only a commercial haven for frontiersmen, but it had served as the rallying point from which backwoodsmen and settlers had marched on the night of June 10, 1781, to join in the attack against the Loyalists at Ninety Six, some twenty miles away.

Bagly reports that he bought the hotel from Agnou's widow in 1858 and in 1859 added the porch. Aside from the A.R.P. cemetery, Bagly explains that no other spot in DeWitt was as sacred to the town as the hotel.

It was here in the spring of 1861 that volunteers of the DeWitt-Donalds area assembled to organize a company that became assigned to Orr's famous "Regiment of Rifles." Here, too, on the hotel steps, their wives and mothers later gathered, in anguished silence, to follow the news of the Seven Days' Battle of 1862—a battle in which nineteen of DeWitt's sons were killed.

It was also on these same steps in May, 1864, that Dr. Benjamin Morgan Palmer addressed its citizens. Palmer, a distinguished minister of the First Presbyterian Church of New Orleans, had returned to his native state of South Carolina to serve out a form of exile until his beloved city could be recaptured from the Union.

It was Palmer's Thanksgiving Sermon of 1860 that had so power-fully defended the southern cause and its beleaguered institution of slavery. Bagly's cousin, William Morrison, residing in Mississippi, had sent him a copy of Palmer's speech. How its eloquent phrases and stubborn logic had stirred Bagly's soul!

On that bright May day, Bagly listened with rekindled hope as the famous cleric described his recent services as Chaplain to the Army of Tennessee and how those "brave soldiers needed the reassuring message of the eternal gospel." Palmer then explained how he had returned to Columbia and had personally pinned the blue Palmetto Badge, with its proud, tiny, Confederate flag inter-woven upon the state tree, on the gallant chest of General Wade Hampton, recently returned from the War.

Palmer went on to speak of the "bravery of all the Confederate soliders," of their "patriotism" and "solemn acts of sacred martyr-dom," and of the future when the South would remember the War as its "Revolution against the atheistic tyranny of the abolitionist spirit" rather than the "Rebellion!"—as the North called it.

When Palmer finished his speech, not a dry eye was to be found among those in the tiny crowd, including Bagly's.

It was here, too, in front of the old hotel, in April of 1865, that

Bagly heard the news of Lee's surrender. "I had stepped out into the street," he writes, "when my telegraphic clerk called out of the hotel that Lee had surrendered to Grant at a place called Appomattox. 'I guess it's over,' he added."

Bagly continues: "How saddened and rebuked all of us felt who were standing there in the street! We knew the blow was coming, but how it crushed any vestiges of hope! All I could think of was that passage in Isaiah 40:2, 'she hath received of the Lord's hand double for all her sins.'"

Hard were the times then and "double" the grief that followed, as Bagly records it. With banks having failed, merchandise depleted, Confederate currency worthless, and former slaves on the loose, it was indeed an era of anxious days and slow recovery. "Many was the night" Bagly's hotel doled out coffee and bread to drifters or permitted them to sleep in the stable or on the back porch.

With many of his era, he acquiesced in the harsh laws of the Black Code that restricted the liberties of the new freedmen. Along with his contemporaries, he too was alarmed with the black man's vagrancy and open flight from the farmland. How could an agrarian South survive without the blacks to till the soil and continue their menial chores? He still thought of them, in Palmer's phrase, as "beasts of burden," as links between biblical man and the lower animal world.

What Southerner did not want laws that would confine this Negro to the land and mete out harsher punishments for his crimes? How could such a morasss of uneducated humanity be expected to assume its place in society until Providence and time had worked their healing miracles? Why couldn't the Yankee see that?

Often, too, were the evenings his friends gathered in the lobby of the hotel. They smoked their pipes and cigars and vented their shock against the Fourteenth Amendment, the occupying Federal troops, and the Radicals who governed in Columbia. What a citadel of bribes their capital had become!

But there were occasions of bravado as well as complaint. Bagly narrates that a prominent planter from Abbeville shot and killed a former slave overseer in the street near the hotel. The man had unduly cursed a black woman and made sport of her mulatto-colored children.

"Don't I see some Bourbon blood?" he chuckled. "My, my,

Bourbon Blacks. Now isn't that something."

"So what if dey is," the woman responded. "Dey is sho' better dan de likes o' you!"

That is when the man began cursing her. And that is when the planter shot him.

The woman screamed but left in a carriage with the planter. No arrests were made, notes Bagly.

Bagly died in 1889, and so his history ends there. But his narratives of the 1870's suggest that the old hotel played host to both a savage and splendid drama, an ever-changing chronicle of crisis and unexpected grace.

A deeply religious A.R.P., Bagly could espouse the racism of his time only within limits. Convinced of the evils of Reconstruction and Radical Republican governments, still he recoiled from the terrorist tactics and philosophy of the popular Red Shirts.

The Red Shirts were comprised of ex-Confederate soldiers and well-meaning South Carolinians. They had formed in August of 1876, and, clad in their red flannel shirts, had paraded in countless towns in support of General Wade Hampton's candidacy for the governorship.

Bagly had voted for Hampton in November of 1876 and was pleased with the General's victory. But he was proud of his son, James Francis, then eighteen, for defying the lawlessness of Mart Gary's "hoodlums on horseback," as DeWitters soon came to think of the Red Shirts.

The incident that Bagly cites occurred on the evening of January 22, 1877.

In September of 1870, a group of Black Northern Baptists had journeyed to South Carolina to found a liberal arts college for black girls. For reasons Bagly never understood, they located their college between DeWitt and Abbeville. Though often the scene of white harrassment, their college, thus far, had survived the bitterest days of Reconstruction.

The leaders of this college were articulate black clergymen and several white Quakers of Pennsylvania. Haters of such urbane and graceful men inevitably were bested in legal bouts with them. But with the rise of the Red Shirts and the confidence of the people that Hampton would sweep out the state's scalawags, a menacing attitude permeated sections of the state.

Bagly was seventy-four. He and Francis were discussing James Henley Thornwell's theology, when, on the evening of the twenty-second, a small group of Red Shirts rode into DeWitt. Their mission was to recruit a sufficient number of riders to accompany them to the black college, where, as Bagly explains it, their leader promised, "We're gonna teach them Yankees and black apes a lesson they ain't ever gonna forget!"

Bagly and Francis had come out onto the hotel's porch. The night air was frigid. The torches that the riders carried created a ghostly scene amid the steam and breath rising from the tired and excited riders and horses. Bagly realized he recognized all the men.

Francis, a senior at Ebenezer College, and laboring in his heart with a call to the A.R.P. ministry, suddenly sprang up on the porch's rail and began to reason with the riders.

"Please don't!" he pleaded. 'Vengeance is mine, saith the Lord. I will repay,'" he quoted. "My brothers, what will you gain? When you fought at Richmond, Gettysburg, Antietam, and Petersburg, you fought an honorable enemy in an honorable war. God has always blessed such patriotism and duty. But whose honor is served now, and what honor can possibly be gained by intimidating God's own servants and frightening little girls, even if they be black?"

"Oh, shut him up!" cried someone.

"No!" shouted Bagly. "Listen to him. You will only shame us all and shame yourselves and stain forever your own cause."

"He's right!" called one of the riders. "My brother died at Williamsburg. We never fought for this."

"'Tis true," called another.

There was a silence.

"Let us go home," said an older man. "Peace, brother Bagly. You're a man of the Lord."

"Amen!" said someone in the crowd.

"Amen!" cried Bagly. "Won't you dismount and have some coffee with us?"

"Have you anything stronger?" asked one of the riders.

Everyone laughed.

Two of the younger men grumbled and rode on alone. "But," writes Bagly, "by the Providence of God, the others dismounted and joined us in the hotel for coffee and spirits. Before the evening ended, we were singing hymns and knelt in the lobby for prayer."

When Bagly died, his coffin was placed in state on the hotel's porch, and scores of people came to pay him homage. The town's chronicler was dead, but the hotel would witness the birth of a new South, a new century, and all the drama that DeWitters still remember.

In 1890, James Francis purchased the lot opposite the hotel and built the lofty gabled house that stands there today. His sole surviver tends the nandinas in its front yard and tells the remainder of the story. She looks out across the yard between the two magnolias and, with a sparkle in her eyes, cherishes the last years of the old hotel.

"Father entertained a world of dignitaries, there," she explains. "But I suppose the most famous was William Jennings Bryan. He came to speak at the college but stayed in the hotel. He was such a large man that Father had to buy a special large chair for him to sit in.

"Father watched volunteers for three wars parade in that street," she nods. "I was a girl of eleven when we watched the boys leave for the First World War. We stood on the balcony and watched them march up Depot Street and board the train.

"You know my father owned the railroad and was its president until his death. He kept a large safe in his office and used to let me stack and count his gold coins."

She describes the wagons that once, laden with cotton bales, crowded the street. She remembers the salesmen who came to DeWitt from as far away as Baltimore. Her voice drops to a whisper as she tells about the night her father hid a young Negro boy from a lynching mob.

If it is a summer evening, near sunset, one will find her by the magnolia trees sweeping the sidewalk. The magnolias were planted the year the house was built, and their height is unbelievable. "They have been topped three times," she boasts with a smile.

On those summer evenings, the trees' elongated shadows slant across the street and envelop the old hotel in a web of dusk. "I've outlived all my family," she says. "I had two sisters and a brother. He was a Navy officer aboard the 'Arizona' when the Second World War broke out."

She glances wistfully toward the old hotel, quiet and lonely now in the gathering veils of night. "Father was eighty-two. He had sat in his office all day and all night. The Japanese had bombed Pearl

Harbor. And when that night the news finally came over the wires that the 'Arizona' had sunk, with its crew aboard, Father rose in his chair, uttered a loud mournful wail, held out his hand to me, and fell dead on the floor."

The evening stars have begun to blink over the quiet town. You glance across the street at the old hotel, somber and solemn in the shadows of night. Even without its balcony and ornate porch, it graces the darkness. Something intrinsic, enduring, appeals to an innate and evasive vulnerability within you. You cannot shrug it off.

You walk home under the silence of the stars. The old hotel has brought you into contact with a reality that transcends all emotions and images evoked by the night. Only one insight seems to make sense of any of it at all. You quietly recite it to yourself as the image of the hotel dims in your mind. You whisper that insight for your soul alone to hear:

*When I look at thy heavens, the work of thy fingers,*
*the moon and the stars which thou hast established;*
*what is man that thou art mindful of him,*
*and the son of man that thou dost care . . .?*

# THE ANGEL TREE

# The Angel Tree

Many years ago when Professor Reginald McPhearson came to DeWitt to teach at Ebenezer College, he found himself enthralled with its legends about "the angel tree." Within several months he had become acquainted with most of the stories associated with the tree, but until he stood that first time under its mighty boughs and felt the awe of the "angel's" presence, he did not fathom how believable those stories were.

For McPhearson the legends became reality early one summer on a wet, misty afternoon. He had left his office in old Philo Hall and was walking past the Ebenezer Divinity School Building when a soft shaft of sunlight burst suddenly through the gray mist overhead and came to rest on a majestic and graceful oak—the angel tree—on the main mall of the campus. He smiled to himself and continued his walk until he noticed that the light displayed a phenomenon he had never witnessed before.

From the angle of his observation, he could see that the tree's two largest limbs soared upward from the trunk in the form of two giant seraphic wings. The arms of the Winged Victory of Samothrace came immediately to mind. He stopped and stared agog. Why had he never noticed that formation before? The tree literally seemed to hover, as if caught up in the luminous column of light.

Although he nearly ruined his shoes, he hurried through the grass toward the tree. There, under its powerful limbs, where the two boughs winged out from the oak's huge, chest-like trunk, he stood entranced, in awe, bathed in that unique radiance that shone around him for those brief, elastic, eternal seconds.

As quickly as it had appeared, the soft light faded, the limbs grew dark, and all became silent under the great oak. He walked briskly back up the slope, passed the Divinity school on his left, and on the sidewalk of Main Street stomped the water off his shoes.

He returned immediately to his office and from that moment on began recording in a special folder any and all traditions associated with the tree, including his own experience. One cannot imagine, divine, possibly conceive of all the stories he entered. When two years ago he suddenly died, I found myself in possession of his folder.

One of the most intriguing stories McPhearson entered involves the reformation of DeWitt's most notorious derelict. For years, it seems, this man loitered about the town, begged dimes from passing students, frightened coeds with his dark glances, and drank "spirits" in the shadows of the town's buildings far into the early hours of the morning. He soon became a sad and despicable figure, eliciting reproach and pity and the frequent scolding of the Dean of Women.

Anywhere else he would have been arrested. But DeWitt is lenient and its townspeople were forebearing and solicitous to grant him any shadow of doubt—of which there must have been many.

As his condition deteriorated, however, the chief of police was compelled to arrest and confine him, for brief periods, in the town jail. This scenario continued for several years until one cold January evening. As the sun was sinking over the Divinity School building and its orange rays were slanting through the campus trees, the impounded drunk, standing on his mattressless bed and peering dejectedly out his cell window, suddenly witnessed that incommunicable visitation as the sun's glow illuminated the angel tree and its powerful wings.

McPhearson reports that the man let out such a long, loud scream that it was heard the town over. When the jailkeeper found him, he was kneeling at the foot of the bed, sober, reformed, sobbing, radiant with forgiveness and new strength.

McPhearson adds that this man became an alumnus of the Divinity School and for many years was known throughout the Southeast as a distinguished Evangelist.

Not all of McPhearson's entries are this dramatic, but the indomitable Scotsman insists they are true. For example, he lists seven witnesses who were still alive right up to the Bicentennial who saw the following. . . .

DeWitt's only bank stands opposite the town hall and tiny jailhouse and faces part of the campus's grand mall. One Monday noon, thirty years ago, two gunmen robbed this bank. They were in the process of rushing out the front door when the chief of police and

DeWitt's magistrate glanced out the town hall's front window and beheld the robbery in progress. The two men scrambled for pistols and prepared to step outside.

It so happened that, at that same instant, a young mother and her small child were about to enter the bank. As the first robber rushed past, he flashed his gun and shouted for the second to grab the child as a hostage. The excited robber did, precisely at the moment the chief of police and town's magistrate appeared with guns on the town hall's steps.

It was one of those dazzling, hot days when by noon the sky's muggy horizon is already massed with foreboding thunderheads and pedestrians literally swelter in the shade. As the second robber made his way toward the getaway car—to the screams of mother and child—he suddenly glanced out across the campus mall and down its rolling slope of pecans and oak trees. There, the sun's fierce rays seemed to glance off the bark and limbs of a tree whose girth he knew must exceed fifteen feet in circumference.

The light was so blinding he blinked and lifted his face heavenward, away from the tree. To his amazement, the thunderheads were capped with glowing blue peaks. He had never seen anything so strange and beautiful in his entire life.

Momentarily forgetting the child in his tight grip, he released the toddler to raise his hand to his eyebrows for a better view. As he did, the child scurried toward its mother, and the honorable magistrate creased the robber's forehead with a .32 caliber slug.

The robber lived to pay society for his intended crime, but, as McPhearson notes, "he probably yet remains ignorant of the providential nature of his capture."

Some of McPhearson's entries may be passed over quickly, but being a Scottish Presbyterian one can imagine the relish with which he recorded the following bit of gossip.

According to the Dean of Women the angel tree is credited with saving more than one coed's virtue. The gentle slope behind the Divinity School and its lush carpet of lawn, shaded by the campus's mighty oaks and tall pecans, has been a veritable lover's lane since Ebenezer College was founded in 1837. "Many is the coed" whose beau has coaxed her under the shade of the angel tree, there to demonstrate his amorous skills or pledge his unfeigned troth, only to have her look up unexpectedly at those angelic arms and retain her purity and innocence.

McPhearson also notes the inspirational role the tree served for the college's supporting church's publication board. For many years this agency occupied an old brick building near the north end of the campus, not too far from DeWitt's jailhouse and in easy sight of the tree. Daily its staff members would pause to look out the little printing shop's back windows and draw spiritual succor from those powerful seraphic boughs. One of its saintly directors composed a poem to the tree.

> O Angel Tree, Our Angel Tree,
> Thy outstretched wings are lovely.
> O Angel Tree, O Holy Tree,
> Heaven's rays shine through Thee.
> When we are sad or sore bestead,
> We look to Thee, our hearts are fed.
> O Angel Tree, O Peaceful Tree,
> May God spare Thee, forever!

McPhearson reports that this poem was published and was circulated widely throughout North and South Carolina and Georgia and that many church groups visited the campus to see the tree.

My favorite story, however, involves a demure minister who had driven upstate from Savannah to object to the presence of such an idolatrous tree. It seems he had parked his car near the seminary building, about where McPhearson had glanced down slope the day of his conversion, and had just stepped out of his red Buick when he thought he heard a voice from across the lawn. He looked up, but no one was visible anywhere.

It was late autumn and the pecan trees towered stark and bare. In their midst, however, rose one tree whose leaves still shone green and whose robust trunk and branches commanded his attention. A stiff wind stirred its leaves and clattered its branches against the bark. A sudden chill gripped him as he heard the voice again. Each time the wind galed and spun the leaves round and round, he distinctly heard a loud, solemn, "N-o-o-o-o-o!"

That "N-o-o" resounded to the very bottom of his soul and filled him at first with anger, then fear, then guilt, then sorrow, and finally a feeling of peace and inner concord beyond any he had ever known in all his days as a defender of doctrinal purity.

He bowed his head and crumpled to his knees and wept in his hands.

Then he leaped up and rushed into the Divinity School to share his experience with the faculty.

Typical of McPhearson's style, he concludes by relating that the humbled minister became one of the School's most loyal supporters and recruiters of servants of the gospel.

There abound scores of other stories. Their credulity is a matter beyond my wisdom, but I list a few of them for your discernment.

McPhearson writes also that it was to this tree that many a bereaved widow, fearful mother, and faithful sweetheart stole away to pray during the terrible battles that reduced the brave armies of the Confederacy.

Here John C. Calhoun is said to have carved his initials, high up on the south arm of the tree. That no one has found them to this day seemed of little consequence to McPhearson.

Slaves are reported to have gathered here by stealth and re-enacted their pagan, African rituals and voodoo dances.

Some say that the Huguenots first encamped here. And there are legends that the Cherokees worshipped the Great Spirit in a grove of such trees of which this is the sole survivor.

McPhearson reports that the year before he arrived at Ebenezer, the president of the college had a team of Clemson dendrologists come and measure the tree and estimate its age. According to their calculations, the tree is roughly between 385 and 392 years old. I measured it myself last year: eighteen feet and seven inches in circumference.

Two months ago a violent storm suddenly broke over DeWitt. It was a night storm, and the lightning flashed from one end of town to the other. Without warning, a loud clap of thunder echoed across the campus mall as a bolt of ragged lightning seared the black sky with a crackling roar. A hollow feeling seized the townspeople's stomachs.

As soon as the storm rumbled away noisily to the northeast, carport lights were turned on, car doors were opened, and the townspeople converged on the campus. Car lights beamed drearily down the steaming slope at the wreck of a huge tree. People sadly descended the slope to assess the unbearable loss.

Suddenly someone shouted, "Look, these boughs aren't oak!

They're pecan! It's a neighboring pecan that got struck!" The roar of joy that went up was almost equal to that which the tree had made when it was struck.

# MOSES WASHINGTON

# Moses Washington

Moses Washington was a poor man but fiercely independent and proud.

He lived in a blackened clapboard cabin on the edge of the Sumter National Forest with his daughter and one-year old grandchild.

In front of his cabin stretched a large uncultivated field, dense in broom sedge and tall pine seedlings. Behind it loomed still larger pines, trees that were ready for thinning and harvest.

At one time he could stand on his front porch and see the distant highway. But the pines and dense growth had long ago obscured the view.

A dirt lane led from his cabin to the highway, a full quarter-of-a-mile away. It curved through the woods and bordered on the edge of the vast field.

It was lonely in the pines, dark, and isolated, and as the trees grew taller each year, he worried at first for his daughter and now his grandchild. He never knew when a fire might sweep across the field and, driven by the wind, engulf the forest around them.

He would move if there were someplace to go. "But where?" he would ask himself. "Where is Moses and dis family goin' to go?"

His one redemption was a small garden patch that he had cleared on the edge of the field. Year in and year out he kept something "comin'," mostly collards, to be sure, but greens as well, and he had laid up many a mound of sweet potatoes, enough to feed himself and his family over the years.

"Yes-suh!" he would say to himself. And, "My, my!" as he reminisced how his children had sucked the sweet potato skins down to their fingers.

Now only he, his daughter, and little grandchild were left. His wife had died four years ago and his children had all moved away. "No. Just drifted away," he reminded himself. " 'Cause there wasn't no work for 'em in McCormick County."

Sometimes when he was hoeing his collards, he would straighten up and stare out across the broom sedge and young pine growth. He could remember when that field was awash with cotton and he and his wife and older children had slaved in it for not much more than he had now.

Of course he did have chickens and hogs then. But you can't feed chickens nothing, or slop hogs on pine cones. Besides, it was all he could do to provide what "vit'les" they had.

Luckily for him when the cotton died out, he was still big and strong. Mister Adam had let him stay in the cabin, and so had his widow and Mister Charles.

Times had sure been hard. And once all the livestock and chickens were gone, they "near" starved. But with the coming of the war, there was more odd-jobbing than he could do. And the white folks had sure kept him busy and had tipped well, too.

He mopped his forehead and reckoned he ought to be glad he was still alive. "Yes-suh!" But the world had sure changed! And he was out of place even among his own people, and no longer of need to the white folks.

Sometimes he hated to walk up the road to Mister Charles' store. For Mister Charles always made him feel like an old-fashioned Negro, handing him down old clothes and things, letting him charge more than he could pay for, and him having to say, "Yes-suh, Mister Charles. Thank you, Mister Charles. May the Almighty God bless you, Mister Charles. I was grieved to hear that your mother died."

But the Lord knew that, if it weren't for Mister Charles, where would he be? "Where would old Moses be? In the poor house," he would answer himself, wondering if there really were such a place.

But then he liked his old cabin and the liberty of comin' and goin' as he pleased. Just the freedom of walking up and down the road was a pleasure he craved.

"Yes'suh! I'm my own man. I don't belong to nobody! No-suh!"

And he guessed that was the truth. For even the brothern looked down their flat shiny noses at him. For it really wasn't so much the white folks who unnerved him any more. It was the young bucks. Fiercer and prouder than the world. Driving up and down the back roads on their motorbikes. Calling him "Uncle Tom," and "old nigger," and molesting the girl until they got her pregnant. And now they wouldn't even speak to her. Wouldn't even touch the baby!

"Devils, they were!" he would say to himself. "They ain't no brothern. They're devils!"

When he wasn't working the garden, or up at the store, he wove baskets. He wove good baskets and derived great consolation from it.

Ellie's baby would sit on the porch and play with the long oak strips while he wove them into baskets.

"Careful, honey," he would say, "lest you gets a splinter." Then he would pick out the ragged ones so she wouldn't hurt herself.

Sometimes she would sit on the strips and suck the ends. "Ellie, that baby's hungry," he would say. "Poo' little darlin'!" then he would lay aside his weaving, take her in his arms, and carry her back into the kitchen.

Ellie stayed in the house most of the time. He often wondered why the child didn't run away. She wasn't but fourteen, and any childhood she had ever had had long since been snatched away. He reckoned the child stayed on 'cause she didn't know where else to go.

Moses was proud of his baskets. He kept them in a shed near the cabin. Whenever he amassed twenty or thirty, he would take them up to the store.

Mister Charles' wife bought them. She gave him fifty cents for the small ones, seventy-five for the larger, and a dollar-fifty for his biggest. In turn she sold them to stores in McCormick and Augusta.

She was a crippled woman and walked with a cane. She had sad eyes, gray hair, and a long face. He never trusted her, but she never failed to pay him cash for his baskets. And that's what he, Ellie, and the baby lived on. "Yes-suh!"

Moses looked forward to the fall, because it brought relief from the heat, flies, wasps, chiggers, and, most of all, mosquitoes. He also liked to hunt, because it meant fried squirrel and rabbit stew, doves, an occasional quail, and baked possum with collards and sweet potatoes.

Sometimes Mister Charles would bring his dogs and hunt with him. They would crisscross the old field and stalk the honeysuckle and briars around the edge of the woods. But since the area was mostly in pine, and neighboring fields had not been farmed in years, food was scarce and coveys were hard to come by.

Moses preferred to hunt alone with Mike. Mike was his dog and had come to the cabin as a stray. He was a cross between a terrier and a spitz, but he would chase rabbits and bark at squirrels. He was also death on rats and kept snakes away from the garden and cabin.

"Yes-suh, old dog," Moses would allow. "You's a worthy partner."

Moses' favorite hunting spot was along a tract of woods that bordered an underground power-cable right-of-way. The right-of-way crossed the highway near Mister Charles' store, cut through the field, then the forest, and led to a narrow inlet that was part of the Clarks Hill reservoir. Here the underground cable went back to a powerline that stretched across the water and into the woods beyond.

Moses knew that the inlet led to a bridge on the old McCormick highway. He often wished he had a boat so he might fish out in the water, where a deep channel ran. Moses would often pause by the inlet, sigh, and keep hunting.

That fall it was very dry, and by winter the overgrown field and the dark pine forest were on the verge of drought. The winter was also cold and Moses' collards were limp and withered. The ground was so frozen that Mike whined if he stayed outdoors too long and the juncos could barely scratch up dirt in his garden.

Moses spent the time splitting firewood and making baskets. The cold, dry weather made him realize how old he was and that he didn't have many more winters.

One cold January night he dreamed he died and was carried up to heaven. There was light everywhere and he could hear the angels of paradise singing. But when he looked back to earth he saw himself stretched out in the bed and Ellie crying. She had no place to lay him and no money for a coffin.

When he awoke the next morning, he knew exactly what he had to do. Only he didn't want to frighten Ellie, so he kept it a secret to himself.

Each day for the next two weeks he went out to the woodshed where he kept his baskets and began weaving a casket for himself.

He measured it so it would fit him snug and even wove a lid for it. When he finished it, he lined it with some old tar paper and cushioned the bottom with moss. Then he climbed in slowly to see how it would fit. He pulled the lid over himself and lay there in the cold darkness. "Yes-suh! It will do."

When he raised the lid off, old Mike whined and licked his hands and face. Moses put his arm around the little dog and stroked his head. "Yes-suh, old friend, the evenin' of Moses' life is comin'."

February came and passed. The first wild flowers of the forest bloomed. The juncos flew north again, robins returned, and a dry wind tugged at the broom sedge and the young pine trees in the field.

It had not rained since November, save for a few misty drizzles. The litter on the pine forest floor behind Moses'cabin was dry for a foot deep. The broom sedge in the field crackled like tinder at the slightest breeze.

Moses was careful to see that the ashes he carried from the cabin were dead and extinguished. He stirred them with an old lead pipe for any sign of glowing coals. "No-suh!" He knew he couldn't be too careful.

Once while carrying a load of baskets to the store, he saw a smoldering cigarette in the dirt by a pile of beer cans. He stomped it out immediately. "Them worthless motorcycle brothern!" he muttered. "They gonna be the death of us yet."

One March afternoon, about sunset, while returning from hunting rabbits along the right-of-way, he thought he smelled smoke. He paused to listen to the wind. The wind was high in the trees and moaned eerily.

He stopped and sniffed the air like an old bear. Mike whined and wagged his tail uneasily.

Moses stooped down and rubbed the old dog's ears. "What's wrong, boy? Tell old Moses what's wrong. That's smoke, ain't it? Yes-suh!"

Mike whined again and raised his paw to Moses' knee.

Moses looked up at the sky. It was aglow with the soft hues of sunset. He glanced up and down the right-of-way. Night would soon be coming and everything seemed still as it should be. He peered into the woods on both sides. But he could not see any smoke.

"Yes-suh, that's smoke all right," said Moses. He struggled to his feet. "Come on, old dog. We'd best be headin' home."

Moses hurried along. He was within yards of the field when he heard Ellie shouting. Just as he turned toward the cabin a downdraft of smoke suddenly engulfed him.

He flailed his arms and waited for it to clear. He could hear fire crackling in the grass. Then he saw the bright red wall of flame and the dense sheet of smoke that accompanied it. The fire was still at a distance, but it was spreading quickly across the field.

He looked toward the cabin. Ellie was standing in the garden with the baby. She waved wildly when she saw him. Behind her, beyond the cabin, smoke moved in tattered sheets through the tall pines. Red sparks floated everywhere.

Moses ran for the cabin. He grabbed Ellie's hand while she clung to the baby with the other. He led them through the smoke toward the lane that would take them to the highway. But as they came around the cabin, he realized the lane was impassable. Bright flames crackled in the trees overhead. Smoke billowed out all along the old roadway.

"Lord, what's this Moses to do?" he cried aloud. He would have to go back. But where? How?

The roar of the fire in the field was now deafening. A lashing wall of flames bore down upon them. They held their arms in front of them and retreated toward the cabin. Ellie began screaming with hysteria.

"Lord, child, get hold of yourself!" he tried to calm her. "Just cling to the baby and get hold of yourself."

Moses conducted their retreat toward the garden. Glowing ashes and burning debris settled all around them. Smoke blinded their eyes and choked their lungs. The roof on the cabin burst into flames.

Mike began barking and crawled into the woodshed.

Suddenly Moses' eyes lit up with an idea. "Yes-suh!" It was as clear as day. "Wait here, Ellie!" he shouted as he threw down his gun and disappeared into the woodshed.

Moments later, when he burst out, he frightened Ellie almost to death, for on his back and shoulders swayed his basket-coffin.

"There's no time to lose!" he shouted. "Come on, Mike!" he yelled. "We're goin' huntin'! Yes-suh!"

Mike barked and lunged out of the woodshed toward the right-of-way.

"Quick, Ellie!" Moses called. "Follow Mike! We're headin' for the inlet! Run for the river!"

By now deep dusk had crept across the sky. Fires burned everywhere. Leaping flames silhouetted their flight against drifting clouds of gray smoke. Sparks fell in showers from the tree tops.

Mike bounded on ahead. Ellie could barely see him to keep up. Moses stumbled behind, swinging the long light load on his neck and shoulders.

When they reached the inlet, night had descended upon the forest. Smoke permeated the air. Behind them, a red incandescence glowed in the woods.

Moses was so tired when he reached the water that he wanted to lie down and die. His lungs ached and his hair was singed. He could see that sparks had jumped the narrow inlet, and he realized that soon fire would sweep the very ground on which they stood.

It was one hope in a thousand, but it was the only hope he had. He lowered the basket onto the water, slipped the lid off, and helped Ellie and her baby get into the craft. Ellie began crying with terror.

"Honey, the Lord sees and hears. Old Moses is gonna be with you. Just lie down flat and keep still."

He picked up Mike and dropped him into the basket.

Moses waded out into the inlet, pushing the coffin in front of him. The water was dark and cold. Mud sucked up around his feet, and Moses lost his shoes.

The water was chest deep. Just a few more yards and he would have them out into the channel. From there the basket would float downstream toward the bridge. Hopefully someone would see them!

Moses' feet were cut from having stepped on submerged junk and stobs. A sharp pain gripped his chest. His arms felt so heavy! His hands were numb.

Ellie cried, "Daddy, Daddy, you're goin' to drown!"

Mike whined and licked his fingers.

The reflection of the fire lapped in the water. Moses could not take another step. He gave the basket one last shove and sank into the water. He could hear Mike barking and see the light of the fire in the murky waves. "Receive thy servant, Lord," he prayed.

Something flat and limp bumped into him. It was the lid from his coffin. He held out his arms, rolled over, and lost consciousness.

When he came to, Mike was licking him in the face. Ellie was in the river mud beside him. There were white folks and black folks all around, staring at him. He could see car lights and the silhouette of the bridge overhead.

He tried to raise up on his arms but could not. He tried to smile but lost consciousness as he pressed Ellie's hand.

Two days later, Moses died. The ground was still hot in the garden where they dug his grave. They wrapped him in a sheet and buried him in his own tattered and soggy coffin.

Mister Charles' wife found a home for Ellie and her baby. Mister Charles "adopted" Mike.

It is summer now and the days are hot.

Mike lies on the porch of Mister Charles' store up against the wall in the shade. Occasionally he lifts his head and stares out across the field toward the charred ruins of the old cabin.

In the evenings he steals away. He slips across the road and returns to the garden. There he paws the earth, whines, and lies down on the grave of his master.

# AQUINAS
# GROVES

# Aquinas Groves

The old man who came to the vacant lot moved in loneliness. There was an indescribable air of sorrow and dignity about him. It was as if he had come to search for something lost, to ruminate in the quietness of the tall pines, and there to recover something that only he could explain.

It was obvious that a house had once adorned its grounds. Now only its front steps remained. They were high, concrete, cracked, and rose up out of the lush weeds like an altar where memories alone could follow.

In the summer, a border of neglected roses edged the sunken walkway to the steps. Beyond them, where the house once stood, a wild patch of pink and lavender flowers waved in the hot breezes and cool shade.

Sometimes the old man could be seen sitting on the steps, staring aimlessly into the bright wave of twinkling flowers. Sometimes he wandered along the edge of the lot, seeking sanctuary within the safety of the pines. Often he stood amid the flowers and stared up solemnly at the shafts of light that streamed in all around. And sometimes he knelt in the back of the lot beside an old bed of jonquils and iris, and there wept and prayed.

Why?

Perhaps, in part, because of this strange and dolorous behavior, the observer to these scenes often took deliberate walks by the lot just to steal glances at the old man. That observer was Jeremy Wentworth, a young professor of economics at Ebenezer College.

How he wanted to interrupt the old gentleman's solitude! To break into his strange and silent world! To say to him, "Sir, what is the spell that binds you to this lot and to these steps and this abandoned bed of iris and jonquils?"

But of course he did not.

One day while at the town's drugstore, he asked the pharmacist, Lynt Clinkscales, what he could tell him about the mystery figure.

Lynt looked at Jeremy through his bifocals and momentarily patted the top of his balding head. Then he stroked his chin and said, "It's too long to tell."

He served Jeremy his coffee, wiped off the counter, and looked across the racks of goods that crowded his shop. "It's mostly sad," he added thoughtfully.

Jeremy waited for more, but Lynt went on back to his prescription corner and left him to drink his coffee alone.

That autumn it came about that, while on one of his own strolls, Jeremy unexpectedly came upon the old gentleman while he was inspecting the lot.

It was on a Sabbath afternoon late in November. The air was cold, but the sun was warm and bright. The old fellow was standing on the edge of the sunken walkway, less than a dozen feet away.

Jeremy immediately seized upon the occasion to speak to him.

"Hello!" he greeted him. "It's a lovely day, isn't it?"

He looked at Jeremy stunned that he should speak to him and turned away.

Jeremy stopped. "There must have been a grand home here at one time?" he ventured.

To his surprise, the old man turned back and, staring at him somewhat suspiciously, replied, "Let's say, adequate!" He almost smiled, but hesitated. He studied Jeremy thoughtfully with his eyes.

There was something paradoxically harsh and humble about them, tender and sad.

Suddenly his face reddened, and he glanced toward the ground to avoid Jeremy's gaze.

"I'm Jeremy Wentworth, a professor at the college," the young man introduced himself.

The old gentleman's lips parted as if to speak. Then he glanced nervously toward the steps, nodded an abrupt adieu, and began walking toward the solace of the pines.

For the remainder of that fall, and on most warm, winter afternoons, Jeremy would often see the old gentleman wandering in the lot, or see him standing by its steps, staring wistfully across the dried wild stalks that filled the yard.

What was it he could not forget? What were the deep secrets

that held him in their grasp? Was it some sad moment of childhood? Was it the sorrow of a wife he had loved and lost? Was it the memory of children on his lap and the sound of their laughter and merriment?

One cold Saturday morning, while sipping coffee at the drugstore, Jeremy pressed Lynt to tell him all he could.

"Lynt, just who is the old man who hangs about the lot on Beulah Street?"

"Aquinas Groves," he said. "Why?"

"I just need to know," Jeremy replied.

"Well, he's the last recluse of a strange family of Catholics that moved here back in the 1890s. He lives alone now in one of the Calhoun apartments."

"Is he married? Any children?" Jeremy asked.

Lynt smiled. "That's hard to answer. Let me put it this way. For a long time he lived with his mother in the old house there until she died. That was back in the 'fifties. Then he boarded most of it up, save for a few rooms downstairs where he stayed.

"Had a servant girl who lived with him, too. She was something of a recluse herself. Caused a lot of talk," he grinned.

"I imagine so!" Jeremy replied. "It's a shame they never married."

Lynt's eyebrows arched. "Maybe not! She was black! Or rather a high yellow. A handsome woman to tell the truth, but still black!"

Jeremy studied Lynt's face.

"It wasn't any secret," Lynt said. "She even had a little girl by him. And she was almost white. As pretty an ivory color as you have ever seen. And you could tell she was his, for her face and eyes had his and his mother's written all over them."

"Please go on. What happened to the woman and the girl?"

"Well, that's where the story gets sad." Lynt patted his head and stroked his chin. "The child was killed on those steps."

"How?" Jeremy asked. "What happened?"

"She fell running from Groves." His voice was soft, low, measured. "I don't know all the details. My mother did, but she's dead.

"It appears she stole something of his mother's. Something very valuable! What? I don't know. Whatever it was, Groves must have had a great deal of sentiment invested in it.

"The story is he couldn't find whatever it was and accused the child of taking it. He began cursing and demeaning her, though she was his own, and deeply loved by him.

"The child became frightened and ran to her mother and then out of the house. She tripped on a loose board on the porch, fell, and struck her head on the edge of those steps. They say she died in his arms by the rose bushes."

"The poor man," Jeremy moaned.

"After that, his black mistress left him. Not that anyone could blame her. Groves himself became moody, depressed."

"It's a wonder he didn't take his life," Jeremy added.

"He might as well have," Lynt reflected. "He had the house torn down after that, board for board, brick for brick. Only the wreckers forgot to break up the steps."

Lynt paused. "Some think he ordered them not to. No one knows for sure. Kind of odd, ain't it?"

Jeremy nodded so.

"I've got photos of the house, if you care to see them?" offered Lynt. "I keep them in a folder, along with the register of the ARP church cemetery."

"How did you acquire them?" Jeremy asked.

"Picked them up off the lot when they were demolishing the house. I was just a teenager."

Lynt walked back to his file cabinet and returned with a large envelope that was fastened with a thin, faded-red string. He unwound the string, slipped out a worn folder, and opened it.

"Here they are" he said.

He handed Jeremy two pictures.

Jeremy studied them carefully. He judged they had been taken about the turn of the century. Whoever had photographed the house had stood in the dirt street in front of it.

In one, a Negro child was pulling a wagon in the yard. A small white baby in a lacy dress was sitting upright in the wagon and was crying.

In the second, a pensive but attractive young woman, dressed in Victorian garb, stood posed beside a tall, shy boy.

"That's Aquinas and his mother," Lynt said.

"Yes," replied Jeremy, having guessed as much.

The house in the background was large but not beautiful. Perhaps "adequate" was right after all.

It was a white, two-story frame house, with a high portico that protected a shallow front porch. There was nothing graceful or charming about any of its lines.

Lynt detected his disappointment.

"Wasn't much on the outside," he offered, "but it was spacious and filled with antiques. Had a floor lamp in the parlor that came from Paris. Its shade was tall, deep green, and velvety."

"I wonder why he ever wanted it demolished?" Jeremy queried.

"I don't know," replied Lynt.

"Maybe it was more than he could manage?"

"Maybe. But I think it reminded him of his family, or of his mother," Lynt observed. "She always wanted him to be a doctor. He did go to Baltimore to study medicine, but after several years he dropped out. He came back here and taught science at the high school until he retired.

"Of course, after his mother died he behaved awfully strange. And after the little high yellow's death, he withdrew even more.

"He taught me chemistry, you know?" smiled Lynt. "He would never say much. Just spent his time writing on the blackboard and demonstrating experiments.

"Since his retirement, though, he rarely speaks at all. It's like he's crossed some invisible boundary, some invisible barrier, and can't find his way back."

Jeremy thanked Lynt and handed him the photographs.

For weeks after that, Lynt's words strangely obsessed the young economics professor. He had not suspected Lynt capable of the kind of sensitivity that his recapitulation of Groves' life revealed. He thereupon resolved that he would visit Aquinas Groves and try to become his friend, for whatever small comfort that might be worth.

What he did not know was that on the very afternoon he had made that resolve, the old gentleman was alone on his lot, startled by a discovery that had caused him to clutch his chest with pain and to drop to his knees in grief.

It was on an early evening in the first week of March. The sun had not quite set. Jeremy had walked up Beulah Street in the hope of catching Groves at his lot. He was disappointed when he drew within sight of the steps and did not see him anywhere about.

He stopped by the sunken pathway and scanned the yard. Old patches of jonquils dotted the lot by the edge of the pines, but no one was there.

In obedience to an urge he had often felt, he walked to the steps and climbed them. In his mind he could feel the presence of the little child and could hear her head strike the deadly steps.

The sun had all but set. He glanced around the yard. Soon the pink and lavender flowers would return again. And even before that the iris would bloom. How beautiful it would all be!

He looked out toward the iris patch beyond the back yard. Suddenly his heart beat with excitement. There on the ground lay a man's body crumpled and bent. Jeremy knew it had to be Aquinas Groves.

He leaped from the steps and hurried to his side.

The old gentleman was lying beside a clump of jonquils, dead. Jeremy saw that something coiled was locked in his hand. He thought it was a snake and jumped back.

He looked again. It was coiled and looped, a long strand of something, caught partly in the soil at the base of a jonquil stem and partly in the old science teacher's hand.

The strange strand was caked with dried mud and gray from rotten pine litter. It was thrust up out of the dirt, yet clasped in the old man's hand. A tiny chain of beads was almost gone, but wedged in his fingers lay the faint outline of a silver crucifix.

He knelt beside the old man and clasped his hand in his. Suddenly it all made sense to Jeremy. The little mulatto girl had not stolen anything! What anguish Aquinas must have felt when he realized that, too, upon discovering the tiny cross that he himself had lost!

Slowly he bent forward and freed the rosary from the ground. Then he tucked it gently in the old man's hand.

## ABOUT THE AUTHOR

BENJAMIN WIRT FARLEY is a college professor and ordained minister in the Presbyterian Church (USA). He is Associate Professor of Bible, Religion, and Philosophy at Erskine College, Due West, South Carolina. He is a graduate of Davidson College and earned advanced degrees (Th.M., Ph.D.) at Union Theological Seminary in Virginia. Dr. Farley has published articles on Erskine Caldwell and George Washington Cable and books on John Calvin.


## ABOUT THE ILLUSTRATOR

FELIX KARL BAUER is Professor of Art Emeritus at Erskine College. A native of Austria, he earned his M.A. at the Vienna Institute of Technology. He came to Due West, South Carolina in 1946, where he taught Art at Erskine until his retirement in 1980. Prof. Bauer is both an artist and a distinguished composer.